Corporate Pimping

the price I paid for my paycheck

Corporate Pimping
the price I paid for my paycheck

by
Lorna N. Dula

Ivy House Publishing Group
www.ivyhousebooks.com

To Joyce,
May all your
dreams come true
God bless!
L. N. Dul

PUBLISHED BY IVY HOUSE PUBLISHING GROUP
5122 Bur Oak Circle, Raleigh, NC 27612
United States of America
919.782.0281
www.ivyhousebooks.com

ISBN: 978-1-57197-512-6
Library of Congress Control Number: 2011928814

Cover Design by Craig Heitzenrater

Printed in the United States of America

Dedication

This book was written in memory and honor of all my loves. It is the product of the investment you have made into my life and the support and acceptance you have given me to become the unique and capable woman that I am.

I give ultimate gratitude and honor to my Lord and Savior Jesus Christ and his never-ending grace in my life.

To my long-time love, my husband William, who told me I was beautiful when I was six years old.

I am thankful for the blessing of a devoted and loyal family, including my finest moments — Chris and Leah, my precious children.

To my strong and determined sister Sharon, who is my link to my parents — Norma and Stacy — celebrating from heaven. You are my anchor.

I thank God for my son-in-law Roshawn and my newest child Callie and soon-to-be daughter-in-law April who God brought to us for his divine plan.

I am thankful for my two living Aunts Reather and Anne for the strength they provide.

With admiration and gratitude to my extended family, friends and acquired family for the love you give. To my "girlfriend" confidants: Leslie, Anna, Lorena, and Viola. And to my brother in Christ, Elder James Sconiers, whose prayers and guidance shined for me through difficult times. Elder Rev. Sconiers, your example in Christ has led many to salvation.

In gratitude and thankfulness for the love and support from New Horizon Church and Dulatown Presbyterian Church. To God be the glory.

And to the many colleagues and employees on whose shoulders the tower stands; you are capable and talented, as designed by God.

Table of Contents

Disclaimer

This is a work of fiction. Names, places, incidents and characters either are used fictitiously or are products of the author's imagination. Any resemblance to actual events or places or persons, living or dead, is entirely coincidental.

Chapter 1

Working in Corporate America was expected of me. I was determined
to make my destiny play out as a successful career woman, among other
aspects of my life. I could and would do it all, and I would do it to the best
of my ability, with all the strength and loyalty that was expected. I was the
devoted Christian, wife, mother, daughter, sister, friend and career woman,
and I wanted to help the lowly while I did it all! I would hold my banner
and if a door closed, I was charged to take it off its hinges if I had to do so. I
worked hard, played well and gave my all. And then, the right hook of reality
struck and I realized that I was just another business whore. The last months
of my career shifted everything I knew as ethical, fair and compassionate
in my professional life. I felt used and discarded like trash on the highway
and it rocked me. I did not fit the company's new corporate uniform. This
uniform of Centrevia Disposable Products gave no consideration to one's

ability, loyalty or most importantly time served. Over the years, the culture at Centrevia had become self-serving and dismissive. It mattered not that many of us worked tirelessly for years to build a solid company, to keep profits high, to keep service rates soaring and processes optimum. Many employees simply became consumable fuel for the machine. When done, they were discarded and counted as collateral damage.

At this crossroad in my career, I looked around and found that many people in the company were tired, disillusioned and victimized. Through systematic servitude, my employer profited at the expense of the exhausted and powerless, who provided the labor and solutions but were afforded little to no influence or professional respect. The institution resulting when selected, empowered individuals determine the fate of others is defined, by society, as enslavement. The streets call it prostitution and as a result, the prostitute-to-pimp relationship is formed. I called it a career and my pimp was my employer, Centrevia Disposable Products.

I surrendered too much of my power to the company in exchange for a measure of success and a reasonably comfortable salary. I am a woman of faith and I know that God is my source. He will always be my ultimate source; however, I sometimes felt that I was playing hide and seek with Him. God is God and He is always merciful and loving; there is no compromising that in my life. There were times, though, when I could not hear Him or find His hand. It was in those times that my faith assured me. I never questioned God's might, grace and mercy, but I did ask Him some questions. He loved me, He would always love me, and this I knew. God was always there for me unconditionally and He never expected me to be perfect. Yet, I was ashamed of not being able to separate my work and personal lives. I was a mother and wife at home and a professional at work, and a dedicated friend everywhere. I allowed all aspects — including work — to reside deep in my heart. The fact was I held too much of my self-worth in the belief that I was a key piece of the company's success over the years. In my mind and heart, I took vows to Centrevia, when the reality was that I was sold and pimped at will. I hid my pain and my shame from all, even my loved ones. I knew all the time I could not hide anything from God, but I found that He would allow me to play the game of hide and seek until I called it off and faced the truth. I was hurt, professionally wounded and dismissed by the company that I helped to build. It felt like I had nursed and raised a child, only to have him turn and slap me in my later years. I was not alone, nor was I the exception.

As is the case for many in the corporate world, this was not just a job or even merely my career. The company was a significant part of my life. I could track many life events around events at Centrevia. My life was intertwined with the company's life. We considered the company to be a member of our family. We prayed for its success, and worked through pains and challenges because that is what family members do. The realization that we were instead pimped out, like whores for hire, hurt. I pray that it does not take twenty years for anyone else to know this vital fact. I gave my best to be negated and found no way to stop it or even to fight it. Why? Because I needed the benefits and paycheck. My choices did not exist; there was no option. My family, like most, needed my income to live comfortably—not lavishly, just comfortably. The corporate decision-makers know that we have no choice. So many of us shared this experience at all levels, comprising all genders and ethnic groups. We were disposable. In my case the price was too high because it almost cost me myself. No one should pay that price to anyone or anything earthly.

Over the past few years I wanted to run and hide like a child afraid of a bully. I thought about running away from everything I knew due to the mounting exhaustion and weariness that became as familiar as my own face. I knew that in the eyes of my family, friends and those who were under my charge at Centrevia, I was strong. But everyone needed so much from me in all directions. I always wanted to give—I am a giver and that is a good thing. In my thinking, only selfish, narcissistic people think about running away from responsibility. I was bound to be there for everyone. If you breathed and had a pulse, I felt bound to service you. I served my family, friends, neighbors, church, colleagues . . . everyone. Even at work, fighting for the cause as a good member of management was a banner I wore every moment of every day.

No matter how bad things were over the years, I would not abandon anyone or anything. On the outside, I was a fortress and my assignment was to shield and protect all, including the entity of the company. I ran, I jumped, I worked, I gave and all along the way the more I gave, the more it took. My employer studied me and knew that I needed to work to contribute to my family's income. I needed the paycheck and the benefits for myself and those I loved most. I was paid to work and, like most families in America, we had bills to pay. The corporate system knows that we need our jobs and they know the power they have to keep us in our place. Hypnotized by the need for a paycheck and the false assurance that we are covered in the event the unforeseen happens, we blindly follow. In our fathers' day there was loyalty in the workplace, particularly for the tenured employee. In those days, time served and contribution were considered valuable. Once we reached high school, our parents told us to go to college and get a good job so that we could work for a big company and live a life of choices. There was protection in the stability of the "company." We would own property, save, raise our families and retire with a secure pension. Our parents loved us and wanted the best for us. Unfortunately, the workplace they knew is a distant memory and the security they dreamed for us has evaporated.

I entered the workplace at sixteen years old when I worked at the County Office in my hometown in the rural foothills of Virginia. My mother's dear friend Louise got the job for me and I was the pride of my Grandma Hattie's eye when she and her friends came in to pay their monthly water bill. I collected Water and Sewer payments and was trusted to operate the cash register in the front office. I was dedicated and hardworking, and for the three months each summer and holiday breaks, I made a difference. I helped people and I earned money to help with college expenses. I respected the job and the job respected me.

I was young and ready to take the world by storm. I enjoyed the workday and as a teenager, the more I worked, the more fulfilling it became. Brenda, my supervisor, appreciated everything I did. As the youngest in the office, I was often the designee sent to the corner drug store for lunch sandwiches. We loved the toasted chicken salad sandwiches and the double dipped fries and drink special on Fridays. We ate and worked together almost every day and we took turns eating and waiting on the customers. I knew everyone in our town, or at least they knew my parents or grandparents. I was

Mrs. Nora Queen, the teacher's daughter, and sometimes the regal ladies would say, "That pretty little girl there is Hattie Corney's granddaughter, Miss Anora!" It was my identity, my heritage and my pride to be known as a good, hardworking girl. We were paid to work and in my family, we considered working an act of civic pride and social responsibility. Honest work for an honest wage and the feelings of fulfillment that went along with it. I expected all employers to like me whether I ran to the corner drug store or on international business trips. I considered it a requirement to be well thought of in the workplace. This was my foundation and my code of ethics in the workplace.

I have come a long way since the working days of the County Office. Over the years, I have accomplished many objectives and received accolades and acknowledgments. Through my work, I was able to help people and make major contributions to my employer. Relationships were crucial to me then and they remain a priority to me now. I was foolish to think a corporate entity would love me. My level of commitment was uncompromising. Love was love to me, and it was expected. Comparatively, betrayal was betrayal, and abandonment the same. I was ashamed of being abandoned. I had never learned to accept the things I could not change. Shame never affords truth to reside.

I missed my parents but I found myself rather relieved that they were in heaven and not subjected to my shame. It did not matter to me that I had done nothing to be ashamed of. Over the years my parents found great pride in sharing with friends and family that I was a director at Centrevia; perhaps that was why I felt so secretly ashamed when I was dismissed from the company. It may sound silly to some, but it was a very shameful and debilitating action to me. Some people are laid off; I was dismissed and that equated to rejection and abandonment to me. The difference for me was that when one is laid off, there is an opportunity for a callback should the position be reinstated. This company was removing me, not my position. Centrevia executives made it clear that they would fill the position, rename it yes, but fill it they would. This felt permanent and contrite and I was, professionally, dead.

I was educated, responsible, effective and devoted and I fully understood the importance of work. My parents did not allow us to duck out on anything no matter how difficult. We were not allowed to own a white flag of surrender, much less use it. Growing up, my sister was strong, determined and independent. I was sensitive but strong and loyal, fighting for the underdog. Ironically, both my sister Karen and I were dismissed from positions. We both held our employers in high esteem and we took on as much as possible with compassion for the underdog. Unfortunately, compassion does not serve well to those in power in most companies today. To the average corporate up-line executives, compassion is the sign of weakness and they smell it like sharks smell blood in the water. We became shark food.

I was guilty of nothing and I had so many unanswered questions. Why was my experience not respected? Why were the blows I took for the company not recognized? Where do I go after being stripped of my career and left jobless? What happens to my family now that I have no income from employment? Where do I find another career at this stage? I recently recovered from a significant life-threatening condition, so who will insure me now that I am unemployed? Trash is thrown away, waste is discarded,

and I was discarded. Therefore, to the company, I was not worthy of recy-
cling or repurposing. To the company I was trash. I felt like it inside.

The afternoon I learned of my dismissal, I was asked to report to the
executive offices on the seventh floor. It was a familiar place and I was at home
there, as I had worked on special projects that brought me to this floor many
times. I looked at the familiar view from the seventh floor corner office like I
had done so many times before. It had panoramic views of plush hardwoods
and tall, majestic pine trees. This was God's art piece on a blue-sky canvas.
I knew what was coming before anyone said a word. I was being dismissed
and in that instant I remembered one of my mentors, Samantha Haskin,
telling me that there is life after Centrevia. Samantha was an executive who
I considered to be the rope that towed Centrevia through several potentially
damaging years in the market place. She was one of my professional mentors
and I found myself consulting her throughout my career, especially in times
of challenge. There were actually three mentors that paved the way for my
successes and served as the arms of comfort and correction when I needed
professional advisory. All were no longer with Centrevia, but they were still
accessible. I needed to lean on them in that moment, for this was a sobering
day. I was collateral damage.

As I was being dismissed that afternoon, I was drawn to the concern
on the faces of the executives in the room. I was almost brought to laughter, seeing the strain as they pretended to speak from the heart. The facial
expressions reminded me of a child who hated vegetables, or those times
when bodily functions are out of balance. I listened as they professed how
they wished they did not have to do this and what a loss I would be to the

organization! It was so difficult to make this decision, they said, and please know that this reorganization decision was not personal. Business is business and although they regretted it, the organization could find no other option. How stupid did they think I was? This was not personal to take my income away, leave me uninsured, and end a twenty-year career. What would they say if they knew I was informed of the behind-the-scenes conversations of three weeks ago? I was informed by a member of the maintenance staff, who was troubled by conversations she overheard. I was to be let go, along with several members of the department, and there had to be a rock solid reason as to why. For this reason, the reorganization of the department was necessary.

What were they thinking as they recited the script apparently pre-pared for them by the organization? More importantly, what was I thinking? I should have been crying, screaming, shaking or something! My mind kept telling me to feel, just feel something! But what do you feel when twenty years of service climaxes? I listened as two people with a combined service of six months with the organization told me how much my service meant to them. Their mouths moved but their words meant nothing. They did not know me, nor were they there to see the pain or the pleasure of my career. Keep the words; this action showed me my value in Centrevia's eyes and at that moment, my worth to them was ten cents less than a dime.

I really didn't blame them. This decision to dismiss me was made by a lineage of executives who knew what I had contributed and sacrificed for the company. In the stroke of the pen and a few words, my Centrevia career was nullified and expunged. The words did not matter, because the action was interpreted loud and clear: my expiration date had come. I heard them perfectly.

"Good afternoon, Anora. After many years of prostituting you, we have decided that we are done. You have nothing left that we want, so we are dumping you in the trash heap with the others. Your creative ideas, mastery and talents were used to build departments, programs and competencies. Sorry, old girl, but we have younger, more willing, and cheaper options now. But before we dump you, we will strip you of your credibility and your pride. Please accept this insulting token of our esteem for your years of service, and we really do not have to give you that. We wish you well in finding a position, especially since you are over fifty, a benefits burden due to preexisting conditions, and the economy is terrible. Bye."

Every step, every turn played through my mind like a film in fast-forward. I was given the tissue box from across the room. Now, was that not kind and compassionate? Was I supposed to cry now? I did not need tissues because even if I had wanted to cry, I would not have given them the satisfaction. It would take more than that to crush my world. I felt betrayed and abused, but I had felt the force of life's challenge before, when the doctor gave the unwanted diagnosis. I had heard the words "There is no heartbeat" when the day before, I felt life within me. I knew pain, disappointment and challenge. This was a detour, not a dead end. It was, however, a death to me and I began to immediately mourn my professional being.

Did anybody in that room want out of there as badly as I did? For years, I made the sacrifices and gave everything I had for this company. I began wondering if other colleagues were being dismissed, but by that time I had reached the point of enough. So with the sweetest charming smile, I took my folder and turned toward the door. I instantly turned back for one last look and a smile that hid the feelings of abandonment and dismay. I could hear my mama saying "Smile, Anora; always leave them guessing. There should be a warning label on a woman's smile, because you never know why she is smiling!" Thank God no one could read my mind at the time. What I was thinking was not becoming of my nature, under normal circumstances. I did ask for forgiveness; I needed to.

Chapter 2

In 1990 I left my position at a local clinic and followed a friend to a new company seeking environmental health science professionals. That company was Thornton Products, a subsidiary of Edcon Environmental Products. Edcon was a well-known paper and disposables company, known throughout North America. I joined the ranks of Edcon as an Environmental Health Data Analyst. As the days and months went by, I worked hard and gained in position and respect within the organization. It was always my nature to be kind-hearted and to be there to help and encourage others. I found Thornton to be a great place to work and friendships began to develop. We all worked together in a family atmosphere and there was a mutual respect between us. I relied on new friends like Shannon and May, who had been there for a few years, to show me the ropes. They, as well as others, helped me as my positions increased.

The company was my foundation in the industry and I worked hard to make a mark. The years went by and I did everything I could to build and develop the processes and people under my charge. At the same time, my children were becoming their own people on the home front. Thankfully, they made good decisions for the most part, and I was there for everything from basketball and Honor Society to band and PTA. Watching them and loving them is one of the greatest joys of my life and they will be the legacy we leave to improve the world someday. Daniel is strong, devoted and sensitive. He brings comfort and calm strength to everything he does. He is not perfect, but of course in Mom's eyes, he is close. Tia is my lovely, energetic, talented, whirlwind daughter with the bubbly enthusiasm of ten people. She is creative and whimsical, with a truly engaged, generous and devoted heart. We all agree that she challenged us with questions and to this day she keeps us challenged. They are our jewels and our blessing from God and Ben and I love them more than life. For them, we worked hard both professionally and in our home. Only God can comprehend the depth of love we have for them.

In 1993, I left Thornton Products, where I had advanced to Group Leader, to take a position as a manager at Maxwell Disposables in Dorian, Virginia. My dad's kidney disease had advanced to the point that dialysis was necessary and I wanted to be closer to my parents to help my sister, Karen, with his care decisions. Karen lived and worked in our hometown and she took on the primary responsibility of helping my parents. We both had promised to always be there and I, knowing the medical needs to come, wanted to be there. My children were doing well, my job was going well and my marriage was not in trouble. It had its moments; it was sometimes difficult, but we always made it through. I took the position at Maxwell because I wanted to be there near my parents and extended family. We planned for Ben to eventually relocate.

Because I moved away, people made the assumption that I had separated from my husband and that really was not true. I would not say that there were not times when we wanted to do that, but I did not take the position at Maxwell for this reason. I interviewed with Maxwell and decided to take the position because my parents were aging. It was a difficult decision to make and, in addition, the position paid a significantly higher salary. Coming from that area of the state, I did know that there could be some concern with my being a woman; however, an African American woman in management in this part of the state was as rare as a six-eyed dog. I was confident that I could handle it and the experience in a mega company like Maxwell would further improve my career portfolio. I thought with my heart because of my family. I thought with my head to advance on the career ladder. I thought with my bank account to improve my finances. I prayed but I never really heard an answer. I thought I did, but now I know it was more than likely not God. I wanted to experience a large company and the significant salary increase could help us, so I heard what I wanted to hear. Ben had separated from the military some years ago and it took him a few years to get accustomed to civilian life. We became co-bread winners when he left the military and I knew that my career would need to account for a significant part of our earnings.

It did not take long to settle into the routine of dialysis and my dad was responding well. He was still young and strong enough to do well, thank God. Things were not as good in other areas, however, as my children missed their friends, and most of all their father. Maxwell also gave me a dose of corporate reality. I worked for a man who made no secrets about the fact that Maxwell came looking for an ethnic woman in order to counteract a class action lawsuit for discrimination. I was not afraid of that but I did leave Maxwell within eight months. I decided to leave and move back to Crampton. It was only a three-and-a-half hour drive and I could be there quickly if my parents needed me.

My father was better — in relative terms — and we knew that he would be okay with the maintenance of dialysis. My sister and I begged him to take one of our kidneys, but he would not hear of it. The road would be filled with challenges with or without the transplant. It was not perfect, but his quality of life was good and he initially went twice per week to be dialyzed. The deciding factor to leave Maxwell, however, was not my parents or my children, although they did motivate me. It was instead due to the trauma I experienced as the victim of an attempted assault by a male senior to me in the organization at Maxwell. We were in Little Rock on business and I had ignored his unwanted advances throughout the trip. He drank a lot throughout the trip. He was out of control and I was very uncomfortable with the comments and "accidental" brushing against me. I wanted to go home; in fact, I did not want to go on the trip and something made me feel very uneasy about it. I was not comfortable around him and his booming expressions of manhood gave me reason to strongly avoid him. I did not reciprocate any of his advances and he grew more and more agitated through the remainder of the trip. I was there for business and this vendor trip was crucial to the products we made at Maxwell. I had always been able to handle myself in business situations. On the last evening, as we were returning from dinner with the vendor, I placed my key into the door to enter my hotel room, thinking that he would continue down the hall to his room. He was drunk — I do not drink — and as my door opened I felt a push from behind. I was dazed for a moment and stumbled against the closet door. I felt like I was dreaming and it took a second to see him standing over me. In that room, alone in a strange city, even as a grown woman, I was terrified. I insisted that he leave but it was clear that he would not. We struggled for what seemed to be a long time and I screamed at him, calling for help over and over, but there was no rescue. More than likely we only struggled for minutes, but it felt like hours. I fought hard, very hard. I know I hurt him because I hurt myself. I don't think he knew what he unwrapped by choosing this person and this day. Suddenly we were still and I fixed my gaze on the phone. As he left I stood there, ready to continue the fight. There was no sexual conquest for this man, but he left with a victory because he wounded my sense of safety and my self-confidence. I had no way to defend against his words. "Look, you fat bitch, I can have any woman I want. You mean nothing to me; you are only a woman." I was alone in a strange city and I locked my door, sat on the bed for hours and told no one. There were no flights out that night, but in the wee hours, I left for the airport and stayed there the thirteen hours till my flight time. He was on the flight, and we flew home.

I watched the clouds and I prayed that my children would never know the emotional pain I was feeling. I was ashamed that I had allowed myself to become vulnerable. I played the evening over in my head and I kept thinking that I could have moved faster walking down the hallway, or maybe I could have asked for a room on another floor. I should have been able to change this situation and never have been a victim in the first place. Head games are not a good thing. Even when you did nothing wrong, head games will torture you. Someday, I need to truly learn the Serenity Prayer. My hand hurt and I felt nauseated. I wanted the position at Maxwell to advance. I hated this feeling; I hated being a victim.

I decided to report the incident to Human Resources when I returned the next morning. Instead of an open, understanding response, I was asked, "Why would an upstanding, well-respected manager risk his job over you?" I could read it in his eyes and I knew that the male-centered network had been activated in the event I reported the incident. I told no one except my closest confidant and friend and I knew she would keep the secret as we had so many times. As she tried to console me, I made up my mind to return to my husband, pick up my life and perhaps apply for reentry to Thornton Products. I do not often condone going back once you leave a company, but I went back to Thornton Products.

Thankfully, Thornton Products' executive management afforded me the opportunity to return and I joined the ranks of the Product Support Team. I was back in a place where my friendships were true and the work environment allowed my talents to shine. I was no longer in Environmental Health Data Management but my core friends like Shannon and May were still there. I wanted to explain to those closest to me why I returned but I could not. I never told any of them and I never told my husband either. I should have. I just never told. More than likely, the man that tried to molest me has done it again to someone else, and he probably did it before. I wrote the account and sent it to the Corporate Human Services Office for Maxwell, but I never heard back from them. I buried it; I should not have, but I did. I heard that the person was no longer employed at that site shortly after I left but I was certain he was working somewhere. I reported it, but clearly no one cared. My family would worry if they knew and I was not going to ask them to take that on. I owned it and I kept it.

Back at Thornton Products, my new position afforded me the opportunity to work under the direction of Pam Turner. For years I regarded her as my professional ideal. Under her direction I was able to make up for lost time in professional development. Pam captivated everyone with her intellect and experience. Still fairly young in my career, I held her in highest esteem and I modeled my professional approach as closely as I could to her model. It was an honor to be assigned to her department and I gained expertise and further honed my service skills. After a few years, I found myself earning the position of manager in Product Support Systems. Again, I was blessed to have an excellent director with the fire and passion that I needed to be successful. Lindsey Cedar was my director and under her I continued to develop my team and make significant marks in the company. Thornton Products was good to me and I to it. I was a hard worker and prided myself on development of those in my organization. No employer is perfect, but the leadership and compassion of the company made the workplace positive. The playing field was fair and we earned opportunities in these departments. Thornton, as a company, gave me back some of what my attempted molester tried to take. It gave me back value in the workplace. I worked hard to put everything in its place.

Thornton's executive management was confident in our ability to effectively manage the company. Yet there were rumors circulating regarding the sale of the company. For most of us, it was business as usual and we did not allow any of the chatter to distract us from our mission. We wanted the company to stay strong and we liked the caring and personable culture of

Thornton. The rumor was that we were being sold to another international paper and plastics products mega company. As the days passed, we watched a parade of visitors come through the building and we found ourselves providing many documents, procedures and reports for due diligence. In our business that could only mean one thing: we were sold. Soon the guessing game was over and the announcement was made that we had been sold to an international company, Centrevia, a leader in environmental science and disposable products. The company was owned by the Centralia family. You need only say the last name and everyone listens. The Centralia name was among the most influential in the world. We were sold.

In our minds we reasoned that the transition from Thornton to Centrevia would be uneventful. In actuality, that comparison was like assuming that because my schnauzer was a canine, he could easily assimilate into a pack of wolves. These companies were as different as night and day, and we were about to be awakened. There was simply no way to compare the culture or the work environment and we were about to find out that the challenges ahead would rewrite corporate life for most employees. Change, of course, is inevitable and often frightening. For most of us there is a natural resistance to change. We were theirs for the taking. Resisting at this point was not an option. So I nestled in to help the employees prepare for change. It was my calling.

Chapter 3

The halls were buzzing and our days were a whirlwind of change. Immediately we began to see differences as the international corporate owners moved in to take over the company. Everything changed, from the food served in the cafe to the grounds and furnishings. The new corporate culture left many perplexed and we struggled to meld. The separation between the Centrevia employees and those previous Thornton employees was quickly defined. We from Thornton Products were thrust into survival mode and that does not bring out the best in humans. Along the way, many Thornton employees were consumed by the transition and we became fragmented and dazed. I knew from life experiences that time would correct some of this and I firmly believed that my ability and work ethic would ensure my survival through the transition.

The day-to-day interactions were evolving and there were some positive changes as the company introduced us to something we had never known. With the new company we were introduced to minority senior executives. I am sure that Thornton Products would have gotten to this point, but all of a sudden with Centrevia, we were introduced to more women and minorities in corporate executive roles. There were four women, three African American males, two bi-racial men and one Latino woman in senior executive roles with Centrevia. They seemed to have a lot of power in the new organization and the diversity was very empowering to many of us. We had not been previously exposed to this level of diversity at senior levels. Sure, we knew of diversity and inclusion for senior executives in the global corporate world, but now it was real and it came home. This meant that executive status became attainable, very attainable. With visible minority professionals, we could dream and see this level of success in our careers and for our families as a reality.

Soon word spread that Carl Newhart, one of the African American senior executives, was on site to begin his transitional meetings for the new staff. Carl was senior vice president of Business Development and the word in the hallways was that he was a confident and charismatic man. Some of us felt as if the Emancipation had happened all over again to see and touch this new reality. We were all anxious to meet him and there was an unspoken pride for all ethnic employees at every level. As a people we felt this on a greater scale when the first ethnic man became our president. In our corporate lives, it was a truly liberating day and we enjoyed the fact that this could be an opportunity for supersonic career growth, now that the trail had been blazed. It was clear that Carl was a top producer for the company and his introduction was made quickly to the masses.

For weeks, the lunch conversation was about Carl Newhart. Most conversation was positive but there was some chatter in certain circles that I was ashamed to say was not so welcoming. I was frankly surprised to hear it even though I knew that prejudice was not dead. Seeing this black man in senior executive status brought feelings of bigotry to the surface of a few employees. Change is sometimes difficult and often unflattering. Carl was confident and had his own unique mannerisms; many of the females in the company found him to be an alluring man. I never really thought of him in the sense that he was "sexy," but many did. I admired him and the more we found out about him, the more alluring he became. He was courageous and brilliant and groupies were starting to identify themselves. He was smart and I felt confident that he would not fall to any inappropriateness. He had grown up hard through the company and he earned his way. He earned it and he did well . . . nothing else to say.

We were soon introduced to a second minority senior executive: Frederick Smith. Frederick was the head of Environmental Studies and Biostatistics. Like Carl, he had his own style and approach. His respect level was slightly different, but there was no argument from anyone in the company that he too had earned his position and was a very intelligent man. I am always pleased to see those of ethnic heritage overcome the barriers and stereotypes that sometimes stop many brilliant people from achieving. I gave him his respect in that; however, it did not take long for me to realize that our philosophy in the workplace was very different. I was often uneasy, very uneasy around Frederick. I preferred not to comment about it to anyone and I celebrated his arrival at the site, as was expected of me.

In order to interact with Frederick, he made sure that everyone understood he was in charge and there must be unquestioned loyalty. Frederick was a man of detail in every aspect, both in his professional and personal life. He could recall every detail of everything and he was quick to state his likes and dislikes. He also loved women and he was very quick to note the special features of women openly. There were no exceptions. As he was a bi-racial man, he was very clearly accepting of all varieties and flavors of female delight. I cannot say that he was alone in that, though, because there seemed to be a common thread among the senior executives of Centrevia regardless to their ethnicity; they were womanizers. It simply seemed to be a part of the culture and the women of Centrevia accepted it and in most cases embraced it as a means to accelerate their careers. Those of us from Thornton, however, were not accustomed to this type of interaction, or at least it was not the rule. Frederick was not vulgar or openly offensive, but his intentions were always clear. "I am the authority, the giver, and the lawmaker and my requests are to be attended to." As time went on, we found that many of the women in the organization, from Centrevia's Mount Claire facility, international headquarters and from our Crampton site, had gone above and beyond to please him. He was powerful and commanded loyalty from all he let into his circle. I would soon find out that the fact that I would not allow him to become more acquainted with me was a large part of my career demise. In Frederick's world, all was fair game and he was, in fact, a part of a network of colleagues and friends that was well rooted in social and professional circles. These networks' influences would soon become like a machine churning on the day-to-day existence of the organization and on many of us personally.

By this time, Centrevia's transition was well underway and the top layer of Thornton Products had been expunged. Leaders had been dismissed and only a few of the Thornton senior executives survived the cut in order to see the transition through. The presence of international executives from other Centrevia sites was starting to become evident and the C-suite offices were now occupied by the new decision-makers. We were learning the rules of the new organization and most of us in management were now told that we must interview for positions that were available. It was clear that those from Thornton were not going to be favored in any way and that many of the staff from Mount Claire would be moved here to take key positions.

It was also evident that some of the previous Thornton Products management and directors made significant shifts in alliances in order to find safe passage in the transition storm. Friendships and old alliances were tested to the breaking point and people began resembling the culture of the new organization. The Mount Claire team was very well assimilated into the Centrevia culture and it became clear quickly that Crampton was considered to be the bastard child who would have to earn its way to the head table. We watched as the Centrevia elite were introduced to us and we were all asked to ready ourselves to be evaluated.

I found myself vying for positions in the Environmental Protection Support Group. The previous Thornton management that I respected was removed like timber cut from the forest. I, however, found myself reporting to a familiar director from the previous organization, Stanley Pratte. I had worked for Stanley earlier in my career with Thornton and I held him in high esteem. I expected no favors and I found none. Stan was a man of much experience and stoic professionalism. He was also 100 percent company business and had been chosen by the new organization to communicate difficult news to Thornton Products sites during the sale and transition. He conducted all assignments with a cool confidence that protected him from feeling the personal side of his task. Sometimes I felt sorry for him because I knew he had a hidden, remorseful side. Soon it became personally clear that he did this job well at anyone's expense, even mine. Stan had the choice to retain only a fraction of the management staff from the combined Thornton sites. At my expense, he chose to keep Carlie Whitley, who was one of the three environmental managers under his management. Under the new company there was room in his organization for only one manager in Biodegradable Studies. It was clear that Carlie's style was more complementary to his and that of the new organization. A colleague, Pamela Raines, and I had many more years of successful service and excellent performance with the organization; however, time served had no currency in the new company.

There were other positions that we could interview for in the coming weeks but if we were not chosen for one of these positions, we would be let go. I interviewed for the position of manager of World-Wide Environmental Support under the direction of Cedric Angelo. Cedric and I did not see eye to eye upon first meeting. He did, however, know that I was well versed and experienced in Environmental Studies. He knew that I was what was needed for his new organization. I got the position, but I was scared to death because this would involve significant travel abroad to transition and to build the new mission. I did not let him know that I was concerned and had never traveled outside the United States and Canada. I just prayed and asked God to handle my lack of global exposure. He did.

Over the next months I became well versed in international travel and built a team which thankfully gave me the opportunity to employ some of those from previous Thornton Products departments that were swept away with no positions. I hired Pam Raines in order to give her employment, as she had found no position after being tagged for release by Stanley Pratte. I had worked for Pam years ago and we had our challenges. This time I had the opportunity to help her, past set aside, forgotten.

The ground was difficult to manuever working for the new international company. In those first months as I traveled internationally, I became very close to Robin Paul and Theresa Cartridge. Both were my colleagues in the new position. Theresa was a longtime Centrevia employee from Mount Claire and Robin had been a Thornton Products manager. We bonded and became the sounding board for each other. If not for them, those first months would have been unbearable for me. Some of the international women considered me a fat American woman and they made no secret of mocking me. Two of them were particularly cruel with comments regarding my weight on every occasion possible. Their cruelty was so obvious that the males in the group would ask me if I was all right and say that they were sorry for this. I am now, and have always been, a good-looking woman but I am a thick black woman and the fact that I am overweight is no secret. Women are particularly cruel to each other about weight and it transcends to the corporate world. In the international corporate world, being a fat woman is like driving through rush hour with a cart and donkey. You have transportation but it is much harder to be allowed on the highway. It seemed that to these women, you can be dumb as a post and twice as physically unattractive, but as long as you are thin, you look good!

To the contrary, we, as black women, are taught that if we generally know how to dress what we have and can accessorize, we look good and do not sweat it! I like to think of it as a gift that our mothers gave us. We adorn in our own style and we are much more forgiving in general if we do not fit the physical mold of the day. That is not to say that we do not feel the pressure; we do.

Food is a struggle for me and always has been. My career, however, was never about my body size or my eating habits. It should be a measure of my intelligence, work ethic and commitment. On so many occasions the international women made assumptions that being heavy means you are lazy. I will remember them and their comments for the rest of my life. I cannot count the times they broke into conversation under the veil of their international languages, as we were known to not be able to speak foregin languages. I did not speak a foreign language fluently. Fluent would mean that I had a command of the oral presentation of the language. It is, though, a well-known fact that some people have a vastly different skill level in understanding languages as opposed to speaking them. No one ever asked me if I *understood* another language—go figure. Had they asked, I would have told them that I did understand three languages and had done several assessments to note my level of understanding as conversational. Yes, I understood most of the conversations and the insults. The jokes really were not very funny and the phrase "fat cow" loses something in the translation. To those who laughed at me and others so often: now that my understanding of spoken languages is out of the bag, I am sure many people are scratching their heads and regretting many meetings, conference calls and hallway chatters. No need to fret. It was never what was said; it was always the actions that mattered. I knew the intentions and I knew who was sincere. There were many fair and open professionals in the organization. In all cultures and nationalities there are people who are committed to positive and uplifting lives. Truly, one's work should speak for itself in any language.

Over the next few years I hired and reorganized my team while I continued to struggle to gain acceptance from many of my international counterparts. Meanwhile, Centrevia was taking a toll on the interactions of people that I had known for years. They were becoming true children of the father. More and more, control, favoritism and elitism were starting to be the accepted practice. I worked hard night and day. On the personal side, my parents were aging and my kids were in college. Ben and I had great kids and our children were much like us. They understood me, and they saw the dreamer in me. Work was hard and sometimes so was life. Ben and I were very different and I was beginning to need more understanding for the mounting stress at work. I wanted him to understand me more and he just could not or would not at the time. It was never about love; we always had that. He was always there spiritually. I knew he loved me. I just stopped asking him to go or do much of anything outside of church and home. It took its toll on me personally and it hurt. He worked hard and gave his all to the job just as I did, but at the end of the day he rested. I could not. I held it in but in my heart I felt a little unprotected. Wives need to know that there is no place on earth that their husbands will not step first to assure that the ground is safe. To be his queen was my desire, not to be a member of his staff or even solely the mother of his children. We just had very little left to give each other at the end of most days. Centrevia was quickly starting a slow rape of so many areas of my life. My heart never doubted our love for each other, but I needed him by my side because the job was beginning to erode me. He was there, just not right there. I took Ben with me several times on international trips, because I needed a safety net for my emotions. I needed someone to assure me all was going to work out. I saw the excitement in his eyes then that I wished I could see more often. He loved the travel; it was rest for him, but not for me.

One September day, as I sat at my desk, I answered the phone to hear the voice of Frederick Smith. I took several deep breaths and began a conversation that would further change my professional life. A few weeks back, a position as Environmental Effects Director had been posted and recruitment was underway to find the right candidate for the position. In another area of the business, challenges in meeting federal and state guidelines were being noted. The chatter was that Thornton Products had made a "hot mess" of compliance at the Crampton site. For years we had celebrated the success of Thornton Products. Thornton had challenges, but our products were sound. There were issues and we knew that, but the Centrevia alarms seemed slightly exaggerated at the time. I found out that there were issues of compliance that I was not aware of at the time. There were also some that were compounded by the present administration.

The company relied totally on Frederick Smith and his organization for information regarding our ability to meet guidelines for product safety. As the weeks went by I had to admit that, as Thornton Products, we had some vulnerability under the guidelines of the day. There were so many changes in government requirements and guidelines throughout the industry. Many companies were being cited by federal agencies due to the nature of the product lines. The fact was molded containers and metal mesh were intensive to manufacture and dispose of at any company. These product lines were entering their twilight years and had not been maintained with state-of-the-art processes and materials through the years. They were temperamental and unpredictable across the industry. The increased scrutiny of the federal agencies, particularly the EPA, was taking a toll on the organization and its resources.

In order to gain control of key processes, Frederick had decided to reintroduce the position of Director of Environmental Effects. The department had functioned with no leader for a number of years. Comparable to a family without a defined head, this move had resulted in deficiencies and lack of leadership. Managers were powerless and had no one to provide the crucial advisory that they needed. The director's position would rectify that gap. The new leader for the Environmental Effects Department needed to be hand-picked as someone who understood the organization from the front door to the back. He or she needed to be a team player and organizational expert. The more I heard, the more I felt drawn to the position.

The facts were, I cut my teeth in environmental science at an Ivy League university. I had the passion to drive this department through the rough spots and I truly loved the people of the department. I understood the challenges as I had worked and managed Environmental Effects before. I knew firsthand the day-to-day struggles from the pressures of management and other areas of the organization. I knew better than anyone how to motivate people and rebuild departments. I also knew the customer support side of the business, and I had my finger on the pulse of the environmental demands on our products. Frederick's organization was many things, but he knew he was not a mentor and nurturer and he had a very serious hole to fill. He was a brilliant man and he came to the one person in the organization who had those characteristics: me. He knew I could mend the broken spirit of the group and that the people would trust me.

I was interested in the position for several reasons, one being the opportunity to become a director. My current level was manager II and director was three grades higher, and meant a significant increase in salary with bonus. At this time in my career, I was ready to make that leap. Frederick knew that. So that day my decision was made and I submitted my résumé and documents as a candidate for the Director of Environmental Effects at Centrevia position. I knew this would change my life; however, on that day, my future would be rewritten and my path redirected in ways I would have never known. Many days of challenges and an ocean of tears were to come as a result of that decision. I have asked myself "the regret question" many times, the one that goes like this: "If you had it to do all over again, would you?" Usually people will answer that they would not change events in their life. I, to be honest, would have made some different decisions. I may have evolved to this path, but I would have stepped higher and walked at a different pace equipped with a totally different mindset.

A few weeks later, after going through the interview process, I informed my team that I would be leaving and taking the position as Director of Environmental Effects. I was excited to move into what was considered to be the first layer of executive management, with all its responsibilities and privileges. In my idea of executive management, I would be able to effect change and help people throughout the organization. I could already visualize the new opportunities and developmental success that I would put into action. On the other hand, my decision hurt my current team and many tears were shed. I would move to the other campus and concentrate on rebuilding the EE team and I looked forward to reconnecting with many of the people from my past years at Thornton. I knew in my heart that the people of Environmental Effects had been placed on the back burner and forgotten about when it came to development and compensation. I would go and take up the banner to be their leader. Leaving World-Wide Environmental Support was a mixed field of emotion. I was successful there but I knew that I was needed on the other side. I prayed about it and I felt that this was the right move for me. I did not know the fight would be for my life and livelihood. I did not know that I was diving head first into a deeper end of the corporate pool. I just did not know.

Chapter 4

People like me want the world to be accepting and we continue to help, hope and work through situations when most people would say "Enough." When reality sets in for most people, there is a point at which they will stop being accepting and giving. I never reached that point; I just never did. I never honed my foresight to say "uncle" and retreat. My sister warned me that people need to have an out sometimes. I never saw the warning signs alerting me against my next steps, or that things had gone too far. I was lethally innocent and professionally naïve. Even on that day, being reintroduced to Environmental Effects as the director, I did not see what was to come. I should have foreseen and I cautioned myself from that point to learn the skill of selective trust.

On that day I reported to Frederick's office as requested and accompanied him to the largest conference room at the site. He had requested that all Environmental Effects staff be in attendance for an announcement. Spirits were very low and I knew that the wounds were still fresh for this group. A few days before, several members of the management team under Frederick had been released at his request. I stood outside the room where several people walked past me, not knowing what was to come. It was almost as if they were going through the motions of dead men walking. I've seen it before: the paralysis of trauma due to events beyond one's control. It is very true that in all traumas, if not treated, the pain will turn to paralysis. It just stops hurting and becomes a detached existence. I know this personally and the memory haunted me in its own way. They filed by like zombies and I thought long and hard about what had happened to this department over the years. They had no idea what was about to happen to them now and clearly they expected the worse. I sneaked a peak into the room and listened to Frederick tell them why some members of their management were dismissed a few days earlier. I felt like I was about to go on stage before hundreds of eager people. I loved the anticipation, the thought of helping people, the chance to make a difference to another team! Frederick had entered the room and all eyes followed him, watching every step. He made no effort to assure or to comfort them and my heart sank. They were hurt, scared and shaken and I wanted him to give them reassurance! I was already defining programs and evaluating the group in my mind.

Frederick was speaking in his usual commanding manner. I was asked to remain outside the room and to be introduced later. He talked about the challenges ahead with the EPA, and the lack of rigor in the department. My heart broke because he had absolutely nothing good to say. The staff was starved for a morsel of hope. I do realize that he had to be all about the business, but

I also knew that behind the business are the people and the people needed hope. After a few minutes he told them that he would like to introduce the new Director of Environmental Effects. When I entered the room, I heard the air come back into the space. Blood flowed into several faces and I was looking forward to working on their behalf. At that moment, I felt like the relief ship arriving at the shore of a starving country. I wanted to shout "Keep the faith; we will make it through!" But Frederick came very quickly back into the command of the room. It was as if my infusing hope into the group was contrary to his objective. It took a few minutes as we literally did a verbal tug of war for the room. He knew I could fight. I am sure he remembered. He was watching me very closely and he knew I would approach this position with authoritative compassion. At that moment I felt as though he wanted to snatch the position back. It was the look he gave me. I could see the wheels turning in his head; I would be a challenge for him, again.

The first weeks in the new position required that I address the lack of confidence in the department and quickly evaluate the services in the area. Most of the people knew me and they knew I was honest and that my focus would be fighting to regain respect for the area. Somehow, though, even on that first introductory day, I knew that there was much behind Frederick's demeanor. I knew at that moment I should be concerned as to what my new role really meant. People at Centrevia had no idea of the inner struggle that working for Frederick caused me personally. I had made a blood pact with myself that I would not visit the dark places of my past professional relationships. That memory was banned and resurrecting it would bring more questions than I could handle. Thinking of my husband, my children, my parents, and my family . . . I just could not go there. My family was living a life that was comfortable and I had two children in college. My husband and I took pride in the fact that we were going to have Daniel and Tia emerge without the debt of student loans. We subsidized family incomes and we were the bank of emergency needs for our extended families and friends. Too much was riding on me; I had to leave the dark place in its place. I needed my career growth. No one at Centrevia knew that our paths had crossed at Maxwell, Inc. No one knew and no one needed to know.

Frederick's reputation and conduct at Maxwell was no longer of interest to me. Maxwell was a man's world and I accepted the fact that my leaving was the best for me. He always landed on his feet. I would work under his organization now because I needed to do so. Pain or no pain, I forced myself to respect that. My professional life was growing. I was a director now and my family was in a better place. I was able to help people on a scale that I could not before. I gave it to God, I prayed and I left it there again. I rationalized and I allowed myself no sympathy. I allowed myself to bury and give no life to this past event. That which was dead should be buried, but be aware that all things buried will stink if not dealt with properly.

Those first days in Environmental Effects taught me several lessons very quickly. I was sobered by my initial review of the cross-functional opinion of the department. I knew there were hurdles to climb and I was prepared for an aggressive hike but not the climb of Mt. Everest. There was no respect for EE's role in the process. In an organization, EE is the department that gives the green flag to the environmental safety effects for products. How would I bring that back with no allies? The battle in my mind was raging but the battle in my heart was even more in depth. Why were EE frontline scientists paid twenty to thirty percent less than other professionals with the same number of experience years and the same science degree? Managers' salaries were also out of line. I pondered and analyzed why this was the case. I could not blame Frederick's administration; he had only been in place for a few months. This was the result of being ignored for years while other departments, including the one I was managing in World-Wide Environmental Support, had management to fight for them. There was simply no one to fight for the Environmental Effects Department and its voice, over the years, was stilled. I felt ashamed for the organization and I considered some of these instances to be the worst type of career servitude.

As the events of this time period unfolded, the reality was that I worked fourteen- to eighteen-hour days, both in the office and at home. I was caring for my mother as her illnesses and age progressed. My father had recently passed away and my sister Karen and I were holding things together. Environmental Effects duties never ended; I managed fifty-four staff members. Most of the people were working very hard and were knowledgeable in the products and processes. What they lacked was heart from being beaten down. When I look back I get completely overwhelmed, both physically and emotionally. Therefore, I cannot allow myself to look back often.

At the end of my second month in EE, we had determined the ultimate staffing needs for the department. We were desperately in need of a manager for the Biodegradable Studies area. I obtained the approval from Frederick and submitted the request to Human Services to recruit for the position. We needed a seasoned Biodegradable Studies manager who could develop the current staff and improve the compliance of the area. I had several people in mind. Some I would have to teach the EE side of the business and I was looking forward to that. It is always good to home-grow your own people and infuse your code of ethics. I had my plan, but Frederick had his. My HR contact was a trusted colleague, and he encouraged me to make my needs known to Frederick.

With the stage set for the recruitment of a Biodegradable Studies manager, my plans were rearranged. A résumé was personally brought to me with a message from Frederick. It stated that the résumé he was sending was for my new Biodegradable Studies Manager. He asked that I pick her up at the hotel and meet him for dinner at Angelo's that night. Her name was Rayelle Flowers and her entry into my life shattered my belief that most women are supportive of the success of other women. Just as I was instructed, I met Rayelle to take her to dinner. Initial conversations, mannerisms and actions told me quickly that we were very different women. Rayelle made it known after her "Hello" that she found the car I was driving to be out of character for what she expected of a director. I found that very odd, seeing that she did not know me. I know now that I had been the topic of many conversations prior to our meeting. I was driving our five-year-old utility vehicle and for my family it had been top-of-the-line when it was new. It was also very clean and neat and ran superbly. It was not new, but it was a great car. I have never been extremely conscious of cars and status. That does not mean that I do not want and appreciate things; I do. It just was not "me" at that time in my life. I was about paying my church tithes, giving more to God's work, taking care of my family and those in need. I remember thinking, *Does she seem to have some type of everyday-car phobia?* Why was she so concerned with my possessions? She let me know that she drove imported luxury cars, as did all her colleagues. Her next comment was that her accommodations were not up to standard and that the hotel room seemed dingy. This was the hotel that we used to accommodate all visitors. The next day she was relocated to a lodging place of her choice.

It was not the Fourth of July, but red flags were waving in my head and the short drive seemed to take a very long time. When we reached the restaurant, Frederick and another colleague were waiting. Rayelle greeted them and from that moment I became secondary to every conversation. The three of them were completely engaged in each other and it was clear that their connection was strong. It was an all-expense-paid, best-of-the-menu night. Many bottles of wine were ordered; there was shrimp cocktail and calamari, filet minion and delectable desserts. The reunion feast lasted for three hours, followed by after-dinner drinks for the three of them and decaf coffee for me. While the after-dinner drinks were enjoyed, Frederick ordered three additional items to be prepared as a take-away. Now I was really confused, as my experience with the company was to be frugal when dining on the company's dime. I realized that senior executives had a different set of standards when it came to spending the company's money, but I had never been exposed to this.

Thankfully, Frederick informed me that he would take Rayelle back to the hotel and with that I could go home. I was so relieved. I also needed to prepare for Rayelle's arrival the next morning to interview for the position. She would arrive with Frederick and now that I had met her, I needed to prepare differently for the interview. I wanted to make certain that I gave her every opportunity to show me how she would help improve the department. I was not going to allow myself to give into the unsettling feeling she gave me. Was I being paranoid? I did not understand at the time that she knew much more about me than I did about her. Note to self: listen to your inner voice.

As I drove home I played the behind-the-scenes version of the night in my head. During dinner I watched Rayelle's interactions and her mannerism when speaking with Frederick. She was mesmerized and she hung on his every word. She drank him, slowly, like a soothing tea. The strange thing was that his interaction with her was not flirtatious or womanizing. It was instead familiar and comfortable. Who was this woman? I knew I had no voice in the matter of ultimately hiring her, and I did not like it. Maybe he would hear my opinion on the final selection. My name should have been Fantasia, because I sure was living in a fantasy thinking Frederick would hear me on this!

My mind was working overtime and I just could not make sense of anything. By the time I had become a director, we were in our third year as Centrevia. Frederick had assembled his inner circle and it was tight. There were the people from his staff at Mount Claire and the people he relocated to Crampton from Mount Claire. In addition, he had hired several people from other companies to round out his circle. What he said was the rule and no one had better challenge that. The few that did throughout the company found out that they were no longer needed in their positions. Then there were those of us not considered to be in the inner realm. We had our purpose and I was trying to figure out what he had in store for me. The company gave him full reign. I needed my position. Somehow it never seemed peaceful in this job, although I tried. God always knew but he never let me go.

After reflecting I realize that my selection as director was partly due to confidence in my abilities and mainly due to the unresolved conquest of the past. The man before me gave me fear. He was one of those men who functioned in his professional and personal life on the edge. I was told by a professional colleague that senior Centrevia executives had a particular affinity for having "fun" on business trips. I pretended to be surprised; I asked to be forgiven. There was no room for that in my life and my relationship with Christ. As a married woman with feet planted firmly in monogamy, there was no going "there" for me. I am and will always be a one-man kind of woman. Some women in the company commented on executives' wandering eyes and invasion of personal space. I was so busy and overwhelmed at the time that I refuse to even hear all the comments. I dismissed talk of Frederick's conduct, giving him the opportunity to engage other women. I have been forced to both comfort and apologize to myself for not pushing it. I tuned it out and worked. I just did. It was easier and I was tired. I heard of women who succumbed to his advances, the expensive meals, the first rate accommodations and the career assurance that came along behind the scenes. At first I worried about them and then I had to face the fact that in our lives, we have choices. Our careers are included and though we all want to be successful, some things are not worth the price.

Work was always on my mind and I found myself both a negotiator and, more often than not, I was on the attack to regain the lost ground in Environmental Effects. No one will ever know how much I prayed during that time. Sometimes I felt so tired, but I knew that the reward was a victory for the people I cared about and we worked hard to build respect.

It was at this time that God answered my prayers for help. He brought to me what I considered to be a changing force in my personal life; he brought me Melinda Dalton and the strength and faith of her husband, Braxton.

Melinda became my strength and she reinforced my own inner circle. When it came to working, we knew our places in our director-to-direct report relationship. I needed Melinda, particularly her faith and her strength, and I needed the nurturing protection that she brought with her. The moment she came into the department my life changed. The people in our lives that cover us in prayer and love us unconditionally are the ones that feed our roots. They stand as our protectors and are charged to walk with us as support through our lives. As our relationship progressed, Melinda and Braxton became my daily vitamin and our existence became so intertwined that my life and that of my loved ones stabilized through the most challenging times. From that point onward, they became family. Elder- Reverend Braxton Dalton was a true and devoted man of God.

The morning of Rayelle's interview at Centrevia, it was clear that she knew she had the position. Her opinions on what was wrong in the department were almost verbatim to Frederick's summary. I asked her what her career objectives were and her answer was "I am open to many things and Frederick will guide me." I knew in my heart that she meant that she would lead the department, not me. Again, I reminded myself to remain objective and to give Frederick my feedback. We went through the motions of interviewing all day. At day's end I took her back to Frederick's office. He asked her to spend some time with his administrative assistant and excused us to a conference room. Once we were in the conference room, he told me what her starting salary would be and the date she would start. I responded that there were still other candidates that I would like to pursue. He bounded back with one question: "Why do you wish to pursue others?" I felt like I was standing before the king, asking for permission. Permission was denied.

Shortly after Rayelle departed for the airport, I found myself in HR working on her offer package. My HR rep and I were both concerned, but we knew there was no alternative. After a back-and-forth negotiation battle, Rayelle was hired at $5,000 less per year than my salary. I was the Director of Environmental Effects and was responsible for fifty-six people and the full aspect of the departmental goals and objectives. She would work for me with responsibilities in only Biodegradable Studies. It was done.

I turned to my most trusted Melinda as a confidant and friend for insight. We had many conversations and said many prayers about what was to come. Rayelle and I were both women and it was important to me to be united. We were professional women who happened to be of color and we needed to show mutual respect and to row in the same direction. I was determined that we would, especially for the young women in the department aspiring to be at our levels. I was going too far ahead of myself and I needed to acknowledge that I could not control Rayelle's choices. I could control only my own and release the rest to God.

There was still much work to do and I was always concerned that the smaller things in our infrastructure were going to make us vulnerable. We created a function to strengthen infrastructure programs like compliance and documentation, training, and surveillance. I shifted some personnel to cover the position and although we were working around the clock, the department had a new posture. Environmental Effects was now the place to be as employees throughout the company noted our progress. Word had spread that I was fighting for my people and that there was growth in the department. On a daily basis, I was getting requests from people asking for opportunities to join us.

Much of my daily attention was focused on the Biodegradable Studies area because there was no acting manager. Rayelle had been hired and would start in a few weeks. Although I was concerned, there was some relief in the fact that the Biodegradable Studies area would have someone charged to lead it. I was busy and there was much to do. While waiting for Rayelle's start date, we restructured the group so that two leads concentrated on the day-to-day activities under my direction. Shannon, who now worked for me and in whom I had tremendous confidence, assisted me with managerial tasks for the area. Her experience allowed me to name her as my designee for the department. She deserved it and I fought the skeptics to make certain she got her due.

The leads in Biodegradable Studies were very bright and eager. However, neither was tenured enough to manage the area and now we waited for Rayelle to begin her position. Most of the activities for the department were assigned to these leads. Shannon took on most of the responsibilities, but there were others on the staff, including Jordan Craft, who would make a lasting mark on the department. Rayelle and Jordan became the focus of many sleepless nights for me. We needed more hands in the area and my thoughts were that I would fight for the headcount and provide the leadership that Rayelle would need to secure it. So we worked and made sure everything was ready. Frederick communicated daily on preparations for her arrival that fateful day. It was clear that his instructions were to be followed.

Chapter 5

I was really tired that morning, but I took extra effort in getting ready. I wanted to look and feel my best. We would welcome Rayelle as the Biodegradable Studies Manager that day. Melinda had arranged for a welcome breakfast, including Frederick and some of the key staff, and I wanted to get there early to take care of my morning signatures and oversight. My plan was to begin her transition training immediately. We had no time to rest; it was time to work! When I arrived, Melinda had arrived early also. We prayed as we did every morning. We prayed for covering and safety, for the advancement of God's kingdom and for the people of Centrevia. We prayed for Centrevia's success and we prayed that Rayelle would settle in and be successful in the department. Melinda and her husband both prayed for my protection as the department leader. They knew that my battle was to rage into a full war. I was a born-again Christian, but for what was to come, I needed their faithful prayers for my success. I truly needed to be equipped, not knowing that the attack to come would be on my professional credibility, personal confidence and spiritual wellness.

Rayelle arrived slightly late and Melinda brought her to my office. We settled her in, took her for her badge and keys, introduced her to the management, and then to her immediate team. It was a pleasant morning and unlike our first few meetings, she was both respectful and approachable. For the remainder of the morning, we left her with her team. She and I would begin the checklist of management training items that afternoon; for now I wanted her to know the people of her area. The afternoon did not go as planned due to some unexpected needs for my time as director. Problems would require my attention, so Shannon worked with Rayelle for the afternoon. There is valuable insight in having a person you trust work closely with someone you are concerned about. The insight is valuable and in most of life, people who have the same goals usually harmonize their thinking. Shannon and I were in harmony. When it came to Rayelle, the leopard had spots and did not care to hide them, nor would she even try. We were in for a ride.

I had reclaimed some storage space and redistributed some of the sampling areas in Biodegradable Studies to make a new office area. Rayelle's position was new and we were limited on space. My position as Director of Environmental Effects had not existed either so an office had to be created from existing space when I came over to the department. I gave up some of the director's office space and we used more storage space to make Rayelle's office. Abracadabra, the Biodegradable Studies Manager's office was created. I sacrificed having the windows so that her office, directly behind mine, could have the benefit of window light due to the location and size. Rayelle informed me that the office and the standard furniture were unacceptable and that she would discuss a new office with Frederick. My future plan included more office space for the department, but for now there was just no option. This was a very low priority on my to-do list. Mama always said chose your battles and with everything on my plate, frankly, this was not the day.

As the days went on, the connection with Frederick and Rayelle became very evident. So did the underlying competition that Rayelle had with me; it was increasing with ballistic speed. More pressing for me, however, was the growing division that seemed to be an undercurrent in the Biodegradable Studies staff. In the initial days, Rayelle spoke highly of and relied on the leads in the area. She even approached me regarding an increase for one of the leads, Hailey. She openly admitted often that Hailey was the workhorse and go-to person. The more interesting relationship that was brewing, though, was that of Jordan Craft and Rayelle. Rayelle was very physical and ornate and Jordan was clearly in awe of her. It took a while but I noticed an unhealthy relationship building between Rayelle and Jordan at the expense of the other staff members.

My interactions with Rayelle were progressing with concern. Consistently she went over my head and around me to Frederick. It was not long before new furniture had been ordered for the office she was given. I reminded her often that the standard issue furniture for managers was not to be replaced due to budget restraints; again my rule was dismissed and my department was charged with purchases without my approval. In addition, the temporary living expenses for Rayelle, which should have been provided for two months, were extended to four months and her sign-on bonus was increased from $10,000 to $25,000, all not authorized by me as director. My direction of the department was going very well in all other aspects; however, there was, from day one, a total disregard from Rayelle.

Eight weeks after her arrival at the site, we had our first inspection from the Environmental Protection Agency (EPA). I had been director of the department for a total of four months and we had improved markedly, but not enough to withstand the extreme scrutiny of an EPA audit. There just had not been enough time to correct years of neglect. But, here we were and we had to perform. The inspection was from the division of the EPA that deals with coatings and dyes in biodegradable products and therefore the concentration was for the products containing these chemicals. We would be inspected in Biodegradable Studies, as this department performed crucial studies and monitoring. Rayelle's group was in the thick of the inspection. I remained in the audit room with the inspectors as the Environmental Effects management representative and called for my managers and staff as we needed them.

It was at this time I found out the depth of Frederick's influence throughout the industry. The representatives from the EPA were clearly familiar with him and the interactions throughout the inspection were beyond any I had seen. This inspector interacted in a cool and matter-of-fact way with me; however, his interactions with Rayelle were friendly and familiar. I had dealt with the EPA over the years, but never as a director and certainly not with this inspector. We got through the inspection, although there were deficiencies noted. We took a hit, but most were items we had identified and some that we had already addressed. The new items were documented and we began to address them immediately. We were not in good shape and things were serious, but we were making our way.

We were working feverishly as a team, but the aspects of Rayelle that began to emerge after the inspection were frightening. She continued to segregate the staff through her subtle hypnosis of Jordan Craft. Rumors were circulating that Rayelle was seen after hours with Jordan over the next months. It was an infatuation for Jordan and I tried to rationalize it as mentor relationship that had gone wrong. Surely, as we were all adults, it would resolve itself. Adding to the intrigue was that Rayelle was beginning to identify instances wherein Hailey, the lead in the area, was not performing well. When we discussed it, I noted the same tone in her voice when she discussed Hailey that she used when she mentioned my name. What motivated this? And why was the Hailey she raved about, after a matter of months, turning into someone that she considered to be unacceptable?

I did not like what I was seeing and I brought Rayelle in for a detailed discussion. Her comments had no merit. Hailey was doing the work she expected but now Rayelle doubted her. I asked for the proof that brought this to her attention and she indicated that she would ask Jordan to help assemble the proof. Her comments were that she did not consider Hailey to be the caliber she wanted in the department. I did not buy that. As I sat there, I wondered what changed her opinion; clearly, if there was proof, it was not available to me at that time. Rayelle had declared a vengence and I did not know why.

That evening, Shannon and I were meeting in my office when suddenly Frederick entered. I fought with fear every time Frederick entered my door. Never, however, did I allow fear to win. We greeted him and began to talk about some of the EPA interactions. He was also there to invite us to a dinner he was hosting. As he talked he abruptly stopped to comment on Shannon's blouse. He told us that he could have as many women as he wanted and that he could have either of us if he wanted. He let us know that he knew how to treat a woman. As had become my routine response, I asked that we return to the topic at hand; I was not interested. Shannon quickly stated that he certainly was mistaken, echoing my "Get over yourself" tone. In a matter of minutes Rayelle quickly came into my office. I was startled when she entered but I realized something in that moment. This conversation was not the first where Rayelle entered my office on cue when Frederick entered. In fact, as I recalled, almost every time he entered my office, she entered shortly after him. Now, I am no detective but it seemed to me that she was listening through the walls or somehow she could hear the conversations in my office.

I was curious with this new information and I decided to work later that night. How was she hearing Frederick enter? I turned on my speakerphone, called a friend and asked her to keep talking until I came back to the phone. Rayelle and I shared a wall and I just could not believe the wall was that thin! Behind the books on the shelf, I found a small hole that entered my office just below the file drawer. This hole was about the size of a dime and I wonder to this day what fit into that hole. What I did not wonder was if she ever heard anything that she could use against me. I did not worry about that because I worked very hard to not say things that

I would regret. I placed a maintenance order and the wall was replaced with a metal interior for sound-proofing. I became increasingly aware of my conversations in the office. Frederick challenged me on the expense but I informed him that the Facilities Department needed to repair the wall for other issues. It took place after hours and did not disturb Rayelle's or my daily work.

As the relationship between Rayelle and the staff became more inflammatory, she came to me with several reports that Hailey had completed and insisted that there were mistakes in the reports. With her she brought Jordan as proof that this was the case. Rayelle wanted Hailey to be dismissed. I did not understand, since these were reports Hailey had done many times. Rayelle always had a mission and typically the mission was to emphasize her cause. Hailey was round and what we call, as black women, thick. My cousins used to say she was built low for comfort, not speed. She was simply a woman with more-than-typical thighs and hips, and she was spunky. She was strong and Rayelle did not like that. Behind the scenes, we later found that Rayelle was aware of Frederick's attraction to Hailey and he made his desires clear to her. In his thinking, anyone low in the organization would be appreciative of his advances. In my position, I was constantly on guard for situations where there was harassment, but I did not see this one. I knew his way, but I was so busy building and shielding the department that I failed Hailey in not protecting her. Rayelle hated her as she did me, and I really thought that her hatred for me was transferrred to Hailey. Her feelings were at the root of it, and this propelled Hailey into the category of a threat. Hailey was a single mother and Frederick knew that she could use the perks that he could make available. I commend Hailey; she stood strong and gave no attention to his advances.

And still none of us were prepared for the story behind the emotions that Rayelle began to reveal. This story went beyond the desire of power or a man and well beyond the roles and responsibilities of Centrevia. Rayelle's hatred for me, Hailey, even Shannon touched the hem of history for people of color. Rayelle's eyes told the story the first time I met her, and when she looked at me I knew that the skin I wore, in her mind, was at the root of her hatred. It is there within all cultures of color. Looming in the shadows where we tuck away our fears and the white lies passed down from generations. It is there between the golden sun-bathed rice field workes of Asia and the elite. It lives as a code amongst many in South America and the islands of the Carribean. It is alive and well amongst African Americans. This is nothing new and at some point in our lives we were all exposed to the brown bag test in some way. I had to explain this to a friend of mine. The brown bag test was, and still is, used to determine if a person was light skinned in a time when, within cultures, we discriminate. Sometimes people applied the test consciously and other times totally unconsciously. We felt inadequate either way. In some circles you were ridiculed if you were lighter than the bag, but in other places you felt devalued if you were darker. Humans have found a way to make other humans feel inadequate by using everything from money and wealth to physical features. We should be ashamed for literally shaming people into institutions and lives of bondage to promote selfishness and to serve the narcissistic need to feel superior. God never meant it this way and won't we be ashamed to find that in the end, the thing we saw as inferior will be the cherished pearl of the raptured heart. In all honesty, it was no surprise to me that Rayelle openly embraced Jordan. After all, she saw in him the resemblance of what she respected. Anora Bradley, on the other hand, was that which she was taught to hate. I was never to be respected by her. This story was no stranger to history, but it hurt someone every time it revealed itself. Women of color making things more difficult for other women of color; shame on us as ethnic women. The truth is that we could all win a small piece of the prize each time one of us succeeds. With the department having so many young women of color, I prayed constantly that we would be the example for them. It was another opportunity for us to minister. I wanted our presence to mean something. The division Rayelle brought served only to destroy. Many days, I felt as though this woman was sent directly to destroy that which we had worked so hard to build. We had not been there long enough for the department to withstand this kind of attack. My prayer was that God help us to be strong and united. Ultimately, God would protect us. No matter what I tried, she rebelled.

The next months were even more of an uphill climb. More insubordination and defiance from Rayelle was pushing me to make a decision. I found her in Frederick's office more than she was in her own and her area was consumed in chaos. I remember one of the wisest things my mother ever told me and it played in my mind like a sitcom. She said, "Two queens cannot occupy one throne. There can be duchesses, princesses and visitors from many lands, but only one queen!" I knew for months after hiring Rayelle that this would not end well and I knew myself well enough to understand that although I was known for my nurturing direction, I was and always will be a strong leader. In the midst of battle there can be no doubt as to who the leader is. I faulted my senior management for not "calling her down" and making it clear that she would follow the order and structure. I talked about it many times. But in Frederick's inner circle, Rayelle had become one of the accepted in a fraternity in which I was not included, despite my position. It became commonplace to walk into meetings already in progress or find undisclosed lunch sessions. Nothing and nobody penetrated the inner core. There was no turning back for me.

In my mind I had begun the exercise of justifying the fact that Rayelle was not working well with me or the team. I had to do something as their leader in order to keep a functional department. The corporate entity gave little support despite the fact that many people had concerns regarding the dysfunction of Rayelle's area. We were profitable and that is all they cared about. I had nowhere to go for subjective council outside the department with the exception of a few colleagues. I had confidence in them to help me determine what to do and when to do it. Unfortunately, we knew that the ties that bound Rayelle were beyond our understanding. As is the case more often than I would have liked, I had to make some difficult decisions. I was prepared to do so.

At the same time, I was contemplating how to proceed with actions of insubordination; there was, unknown to me, a movement to dismiss Frederick. Our EPA woes were continuing and we were working around the clock. The day Frederick was dismissed was a strange mixture of ultimate calm and undercover chaos. There was no pomp and circumstance, but instead a backdoor dismissal. He was given a very generous severance package and shown the door. We gathered the managers and helped them understand that even though Frederick was not with us any longer, our mission would continue. Rayelle was distraught about his dismissal and left for the day. I would be lying if I said that I did not hope against hope that she would resign for the sake of the department. The company hired a Fletcher Paper Corporation senior executive with a "take charge, no nonsense" reputation to take the position and I was nervous about a new boss at this point. I was somewhat relieved, but still the anticipation was making me anxious. We were introduced to Samantha Stone and I liked her immediately. She was different but very open to the opinions of others and I appreciated that.

Immediately, Samantha began to build her team, since recent departures had left some key openings. A number of people who had worked well with Samantha at Fletcher Paper joined her now at Centrevia. She also introduced us to a number of advisors to help us address our challenges. I found her to be fair and she encouraged me to continue with the competency and improvements that we had started. Rayelle remained in her position until Samantha was soundly in place and then I made my request to dismiss her based on the continued hostile environment she fueled. With the protection Rayelle had been accustomed to no longer in place, the opportunity was available for me to make my case to Samantha for insubordination and performance. I was justified to let her go and I was definitely armed to do it. We had examples of her lack of respect and the poor performance of her area as to make our case. Rayelle was still causing division in the area and the insubordination was worse than ever. One day, I made my decision that I could take no more. It had come to my attention that Rayelle took selected staff out to lunch and gave them gifts, for which I found "expensed item" reports. Jordan Craft and two others were taken to a nice lunch while the other staff was left behind. Each was given a gift and a gift card as a thank you for a job well done. The other staff members brought this to my attention when the foursome returned from lunch. In my mind this was grounds for immediate dismissal. For the rest of that afternoon, I gathered the facts and reviewed expense reports to see if there were any questionable items. When everyone had left for the day, I decided to leave earlier than usual, as I was simply exhausted and aggravated. My routine was to stay long after the department staff in order to prepare for the next day.

In my mind, I could not rationalize why Rayelle seemed to thrive on divisiveness. Why make the environment so hostile? In addition, her peers and others in the company were uncomfortable around her. Every day there was another report of her attitude in meetings and other forums. Half way home, I realized that my cell phone was not in the holder and subsequently found that it was not in my purse. A quick turnaround and I was headed back to my office. The parking lot was virtually empty and I noticed that Rayelle's car was still there. I really did not want to run into her, as I was still very agitated due to her latest action with the staff. I just needed to go home that night and decompress a moment. Melinda was already gone, but I noticed that the light was on in our office. I thought for a moment that I had left it on or maybe the housekeeping staff had forgotten to turn it off. As I approached the door, Rayelle came out of the office. We looked eye to eye with an intense exchange of energy. It was as though the world stood still and the next person to move would forever be declared the stronger one.

I was taught that in a moment like this, the next person to speak is the loser. So I locked in and said nothing. Rayelle spoke in a distinctive voice. "Good evening, Anora." She told me she needed something from Melinda's desk.

I gave her a very cool, "Oh, and what exactly did you need?"

No sooner than she finished the statement, Jordan Craft came out of the door with so much excitement he almost knocked me down. He was practically giggling with excitement. My skin crawled, because I knew that the two of them typically were responsible for things that would either contribute to someone's pain or perhaps result in the loss of someone's credibility and/or position. In that moment, I was beginning to get really concerned. After all, I was responsible for the success of the department. I informed Rayelle that no one was to enter the director's office area after hours. Thankfully, I was the type of person that never left anything out in the open, but I later found out that she was sorting through my mail on a regular basis and previewing any incoming mail in the inbox. I remembered, "No weapon formed against me will prosper." I thank God for that word directly from the Bible.

The conversation I was having with myself went like this: let her look, let her dishonor and disrespect my position and let her think that I would be too weak to let her go. She was very wrong. With the agreement of Samantha and with the proper approvals from HR, I dismissed Rayelle three days later. She informed us as we read the dismissal that she would guarantee I was going to "go down." Her words were short and cold. Frankly, I did not care to hear anything else. She was to leave the premises immediately. We did allow her to return to her office for a few personal items and I regret that I did not accompany her personally. I knew that my future would more than likely include hearing from her on some level. But I had to put this decision in its place and try everything I could to resurrect order to the area under Rayelle's charge. I refused to believe that we could not mend the riff and reunited the staff under my interim, and soon another manager's charge. Concerns were great that with Jordan Craft left behind, Rayelle's influence would still be present. I knew they were seeing each other outside of the office and to Jordan the risk was worth it. Of course, he did not have the means or the depth to make my life as uncomfortable as Rayelle and it did not take long for him to reveal his intent to avenge his mentor.

I took over the management while we recruited a new manager and on the surface, the staff seemed to begin to heal. We were working hard to correct deficiencies, relying on contracted advisors for help. They were from some of the best-known firms in the country. Night and day it seemed that advisors were at the site working with us on corrective actions. As we dug deeper into the area's operations, it was revealed that Jordan Craft was of questionable professional ethics. It was evident and unmistakable. All that time, Rayelle used Jordan to create the story to incriminate others. Now it was revealed that it was definitely Jordan all along. I launched an investigation and spent many days showing the consequences that Rayelle and Jordan's plan had caused.

The advisors from Medlin Price, one of our consultant firms, walked me through more investigations and with each turn I became more and more convinced that dismissing Rayelle was not only necessary but absolutely freeing to the remaining staff. It was not long before Jordan and other reminders of Rayelle were gone. I was very thankful. The problem was that the extent of her hatred for me gave birth to more hatred. We closed our ranks as best we could and began to pray. Big issues were coming and big guns would be required. I was tired and so was the staff. We did not stop working. There was no time for rest now.

Chapter 6

It only took a few months before representatives from the EPA came back to finish the job they started in the last audit. From the moment they entered the building, it was clear that they came with a mission. I found out that they actually came with two missions: one for the organization and one for me. It was obvious to all of us who knew the history of Centrevia's recent years that the EPA had some prompting from either a former or current employee. We suspected that a complaint of some sort was behind this drop-in visit. I was confident in the fact that despite the issues we had, the areas under my charge had no hidden agendas. I believed in truth and transparency but we knew that everyone in the organization did not and we were still recovering.

As the leader of Environmental Effects, I knew where the issues were and I had brought the attention of the organization to those in my area. My direct reports knew that they had full access to act when they noted concerns or anything questionable. Unfortunately, I was not considered to tow the company line by some senior executives. But I did have an ally in my direct executive, Samantha Stone. Perhaps this was because she knew some of what I faced as a woman in the business, or maybe it was just because she knew the importance of getting to know managers before you condemn and deflate them. I was viewed as someone that caused delays and functioned in a too cautious mode. Frankly, I just preferred not to wait to make decisions that led to product or customer consequences, so a few extra hours of waiting were worth it.

Samantha had brought new management to the team and she was either respected much or hated throughout the organization. She was not perfect, and as often happens with strong women, she was considered to be opinionated and challenging. Whatever she was, she was fair, well informed and she gave me the chance I needed to turn my area around. From those not in my corner, I heard over and over that "this is a business." I often wondered why I needed to be reminded of this considering I had successfully built departments, was degreed by two universities, one Ivy League, and knew the organization's needs. I knew the regulations but more importantly I knew myself and my standards.

I was confident that in Environmental Effects, we did everything in our power to represent Centrevia well in the industry. We had issues but we faced them. As anyone who understands the structure of our business knows, I had direct responsibility as the director, but others in management positions had power to override me in the organizational chart. I knew for sure that my organization did its job, and yet I was accused by some of not being technical enough, missing the big picture and so many other accusatory insults. My team was often ridiculed but the truth was that we were sound and knowledgeable and we afforded the organization many successes. It took time to rebuild this department.

For several months, the company allowed Environmental Effects to report to the Finance Organization. This should never be the case, due to conflict of interest and lack of impartiality. When the financial area polices and monitors the policies of areas outside of finance, expect issues and conflicts. The executive management knew that this was not an optimal arrangement, but it served the purpose of keeping the bottom line in the black. When issues were raised, the authority was stripped from Environmental Effects and the decision was made by executives of Finance. The addition of the director's position was a step in the right direction. Furthermore, now that Samantha was hired as senior executive, we regained executive authority to stand on our decisions. I was never the kind of person to negate my duties. I did not do it through the Frederick years, and I was not about to do it ever. Samantha fought to keep our authority. Many things were said about her, but unmistakably she fought to keep the power of our role in spite of the other executives' pressure around her.

Samantha had brought with her, from her previous company, several professionals. One of them was Randall Patterson, our new Director of Policies and Standards. It was clear to me that although there was a mutual respect for Randall, there were some loose floorboards in their relationship. As the initial days went by, it became increasingly noticeable that the relationship between Randall and a few of his direct reports were inappropriate. There is a familiarity that people have when their relationship transcends the realm of professional, and it is noticeable. I left this alone because the rumor mill was aflutter with stories of people witnessing inappropriate events. Randall was my colleague and peer, and under Samantha's organization we had much work to do as a team. It was noted that, on occasion, Randall's decisions were often clouded by his need to micromanage and his quest to be powerful. He would not recognize it, but his lapses in judgment were known through layers of the organization. He had his own definition of appropriate.

As the months passed, Randall and I did not see eye to eye on much of anything. I found him to be somewhat self-serving and he tended to insist that my organization take more chances than I was comfortable with. I tended to be conservative and he insisted that we could justify risks. I have never been a high-stakes gambler and I found it unsettling. However, to the organization, he was successful and in the structure he trumped me. Randall was persuasive and found ways to have his underlings take responsibility so that his hands stayed clean. It was beyond my control. I could only keep my direct reports shielded and continue to improve the department. My saving grace was that Samantha was still in her executive role and would rope him in when he went too far.

On that day the EPA came back to Centrevia, there were three auditors. I had gone through audits in the past, but this time was totally different. Even though the other audits were not pleasant, the treatment had always been professional and not personal toward anyone. This time was a completely different experience, from the introductions to the closing. The lead auditor was direct but fair in his interactions; however, one auditor, Martin, made it clear that he came for several different reasons. Immediately after the opening, he asked me to provide a report of environmental exposure data. I was unaware of a report that showed exactly what he was asking for, so I asked my managers to pull the information that he requested. When the report was given to him, he turned directly to me with the senior executives and others in the room and flashed his credentials from the EPA. I will never forget the words and tone he used nor the look in his eyes. He said, "As a representative of the government, I will have you arrested if you do not provide this report." What just happened here? I was perplexed.

Again, I tried to give him what he wanted and although all the information he asked for was on the report, it did not meet his criteria. I could not help but notice that he was comparing the report to something he had in his notebook. I was asked to go to a room away from the other Centrevia associates where the auditor and Samantha discussed why the auditor was treating me with such disrespect. The discussion went on for a while and finally he stated that if he did not get what he wanted I would be taken under authority. I asked with all sincerity to please show me what he was referring to. He allowed me to look at the papers from his folder, and finally, I knew what it was that he was looking for. It was not a formal report; instead it was an internal log that we used for daily stand-up review. I retrieved a log to make certain that he was satisfied. Red flags were raised as to how an internal, informal tracking sheet would be in his possession. We had nothing to hide, so we moved on. But we were transparent.

The backdoor machine at one of our advisory firms was well connected and we found out that the EPA had returned to audit us based on a report from a former employee. I remembered that Rayelle had told me before she left that she would find a way to take me down. We found out that it was a former employee and suspected it was Rayelle. What I did not realize was the connection she had to the agency was through her family. Martin was there to avenge on Rayelle's behalf. I had never been exposed to this kind of network. But I did know the power of family loyalty and in most cases families are there for whatever it takes. I was a citizen of a corporate community and I took pride in that, but I was also a citizen with confidence in the truth. There was nothing I could do and it was not to the company's advantage to reveal that I knew about Rayelle's connection. Centrevia was under audit, but this time the auditors also focused on the woman who ran Environmental Effects and had dismissed Rayelle, and that was me! It was clear that no matter what I said or did, I was targeted. For additional strength I turned to Melinda, Shannon and a few close colleagues for courage and favor from God. Under no circumstances would I trouble my family at this time. It took days before I opened up to Ben one night after going to bed at 3AM. I had to tell him and, to my surprise and relief, he listened to everything in amazingly accurate detail.

At every turn, there was a surprise but to the credit of my staff, they hung in there with me despite the accusations and abuse. Samantha did all she could to help us fight. In all her years of experience in the industry, she had never seen a federal agency representative go after a person like she witnessed with me. It was clearly beyond professional understanding. I had released Rayelle due to insubordination and performance and I proved that to the company. With her gone, the improvements were notable in the area. The auditors asked to interview the staff of the area individually, without me being present. I had nothing to hide and we did agree to have an HR representative present, along with another member of management. Rayelle had called the agency and indicated that there were indiscretions within the Environmental Effects department. She also convinced them that the staff of Environmental Effects was ill-suited for running and managing the department. My career and reputation were center stage and neither I nor the staff had done anything to deserve this. It was my duty to remain calm and work through this attack; I had the truth on my side.

It is a debilitating thing when you are being victimized professionally and to make matters worse, some members of Centrevia's management and senior management staff began to treat me as if I was contagious. I was the topic of so many jeers and mean-spirited comments, and to my surprise the ring leader of these discussions appeared to be Randall Patterson, my peer. The next day, my character was tested not only by the agency but also by the organization that I longed to support me. Had I not earned its support? Stress and suspicion were high and the days were long. I was experiencing another wake-up call concerning the double standard of Centrevia. While I stood naked in front of a firing squad, most people were turning their backs on me and my department. I gave it to God.

Many things were happening during this time and my world was spinning. An offer had been made to a new manager to replace Rayelle, but it was too early to put her on the hot seat. I took the heat for it all. It did not matter what I defended or what evidence we brought forth. Environmental Effects and a few other areas were definitely the focus. The result of the audit indicated that the system failed in several areas of the organization and that the system was inadequate in others. After all those weeks and all that attack, they could not, however, find evidence of any wrongdoing on my behalf, personally or professionally, and my résumé stood on its own. The organization was cited with many deficiencies and I owned many of them in my area. It was a devastating report and many calls came from the organization to place blame. My head was one slated to roll and I suspected action. No one fought on my behalf, with the exception of Samantha. I thank her for her confidence and the poise she showed through this time of absolute hell.

At the time of the inspection, it became known that Rayelle was suing the company for wrongful termination for millions. She clearly named and directed the action toward me and my executive line. I was concerned for my family, as I was juggling all things on the home front and the difficulties at work. Rayelle was connected to a machine that, after all, had infiltrated one of our government agencies. How could I not be concerned when the threat of arrest was thrown in my face for nothing more than "avenging family"? I was standing in the middle of a war zone under professional and personal attack. I was a marked woman, in their eyes. I held out that the company would remain fair after all the dust had settled. Now, I did not say that I had known the company to always be fair. This company had many secrets and there was protection for those who aligned them- selves under the right people. My problem was partially that I never played that game very well. I was too honest and I fought too much for the underdog rather than for those in the dog show. The company would only go so far to defend or protect me in this case. I learned to stand and sometimes I learned to just play dead. Sometimes I was not playing; I felt like I was dying.

When you are beaten and bewildered by accusations, playing dead is sometimes survival. I did, however, need to protect myself and my family in the event the company was not going to be there for me. I thank God for the ability to see this as a premonition. For this reason I retained legal counsel and security for myself and my family. Most people do not know, but there were several acts of vandalism on some of my property at the time. My outside advisors steered me through the most difficult year by remaining calm. We were being watched and I was relieved for my family's sake that I did what I had to do. I just did not trust anyone associated with the network Rayelle had put in place, so I had to act. Off-duty security for my children at their universities, watchful eyes at home, and protective items for all of us were very expensive. This cost us our savings and we had to be very cautious with money. We were paying tuition for two children in college and with these legal and protection fees, we were not able to buy new cars, the larger home we wanted, and other items. I had to make choices. We chose only our church tithes, charitable love gifts and our family. We had no luxuries. Rayelle had cost me so much, including my financial gains. God made it work.

The aftermath of the inspection yielded many casualties. I fully expect-ed on most days to be one of them, and I am sure the behind-the-scenes discussions were to get rid of me. I inherited a messy department with many deficiencies, which was later infiltrated by Rayelle and her machine. I was addressing the concerns. For the most part, the other staff members were devoted people and the many comments and insults were not true,

nor were they deserved. The department took many hits and as all directors do, I was forced to make some very difficult organizational decisions.
The mountain of deficiencies that the EPA noted was taking its toll and
we were exhausted. My department, though worn, stood together and
addressed the concerns.

It had been a tough few years but we did the best we could. We worked
and we had a few moments to come together as a department to celebrate
what we knew as the EE Family. It was always very moving to me when
my department came together for events or meetings and Melinda, Shannon and I made sure that there was always a family feeling of acceptance
and celebration for what we had accomplished. It was needed and people
were working hard. We gave to each other and we loved each other. As the
leader I was looked down on by other managers for giving the personal
touch to my department. In the midst of the storm we found our strength
in each other and ultimately in the greater being. I never understood why
many in management believed that we could not be both profitable and
employee-focused. After all, there were companies that managed both. I
was determined that inside my control, that would be the case. We survived
this storm weary but holding to each other. Samantha was there for us.

For the next year, we continued to make progress. It seemed as though
we were starting to get some rest and then the surprise decision was made
to release Samantha from the organization. I wondered sometimes exactly
why she was released, particularly since our compliance situation was better
than the years before. There was so much going on behind the scenes and
I knew that Randall Patterson was at the root of her dismissal. Samantha

was mentor to Randall and brought him to the site, but the admiration was shallow on the other end. Randall was out for glorification and acclaim for himself. He wanted to become bigger than Samantha's organizational structure would allow. I was mistakenly copied on a confidential e-mail that focused on Samantha's negative qualities and I found that the male-centered executive committee, along with Randall, had identified this list. Her peers did nothing to stand on her behalf and shortly she was gone. We were devastated. It was, however, not a new event. She worked with everything in her power to improve the organization and then was cast out of the boat in spite of her contribution. Pimped and disposed of; it was a vision of what was to come for me. I just did my job from that point on. Randall, on the other hand, was on his seductive mission.

I could not help but reflect on the organization's double standards and lack of ethics. Why now? Why Samantha? I was sure that Randall was directly responsible and I thought about the lapses in judgment that he was known for. He had been arrested for an unknown indiscretion recently, and Samantha had to go bail him out and helped him regain composure. I had a lot of sympathy for her, as she was the only executive that never left me out to dry and maintained her confidence in my innocence. Randall on the other hand was but one of the Centrevia executives with a criminal record. There were executives with arrests for domestic violence, DWI, shoplifting, not to mention the affairs with other employees. These were violations of the Code of Conduct. Yet the innocent one is let go?

Without Samantha in the power seat, I knew that the organization would transfer authority at our site to Randall, affording him a "blank check" approach for the site. Randall was now in a position to make changes and after a few one-on-one meetings it was clear that my accomplishments on behalf of the company meant nothing, nor did the sacrifices. In his eyes I slowed down the process by questioning and refusing to make concessions. The writing was on the wall and I knew that my personal and professional ethics were not going to be aligned with his philosophy. I was not sure what I would do and I was still recovering.

It was about that time I was approached by a senior executive for consideration of a newly created position. The position was to head a Public Interactions area within the Public Relations Department. The job description was centered in building programs and making opportunities available for diverse and sound Public Interactions practices, internal and external. I loved people and was a champion for them. The announcement was to be made that my department would report to Randall Patterson and I just could not compromise to do that. So, after much thought and discussion with my husband, I chose to pursue the position with Public Relations and Communications as Director of Public Interactions. It was almost too good to be true. Later, I found out that it was. This carrot was dangled to me in order to move me out of the Environmental Effects area, where Randall had expressed to executive management that he wanted me out. I am ashamed to say that the company knew me well enough to know that I would not work for him. They also knew that I needed my job and would definitely take a position where I thought I could make a difference to people.

I was convinced that my years of experience and knowledge of the industry, coupled with my diverse background, were all needed in the position. What I did not know when I took the position was that two people had been let go in order to rearrange for this headcount. I was not told this until I had agreed to take the new position and it disturbed me. It also reinforced the fact that Centrevia executive management made what they wanted to happen a reality at anyone's expense. I was promised staffing to perform the necessary duties and the headcount to build a world-class department. The reality was that once I was the prize cow who ate the feed, innocent people were let go. The total function was to be performed by me with no staff. I found it both insulting and ironic. Yet I was out of Randall's organization and I kept my salary.

I was determined to make it work and I knew that I would have to fight to get the headcount. I was prepared to do just that. I never ran from a fight and that day was not going to be the first. So I communicated with the Environmental Effects Department that I was taking the position in Public Relations and we began the tearful journey of separation. I did not want to go, but I knew that Randall was going to find a way to make things difficult. I was not what he wanted and we all knew that. On the higher level of ethics, it was my decision to leave because I disagreed with his philosophy. I would not work under someone I did not respect. I lied; I had done it before, I could do it no longer. After surviving the past few years, I preferred not to hitch my wagon to Randall's team.

I was afraid for Environmental Effects and I began to recruit for the new Director to replace me. I narrowed the candidates down and passed them to Randall for his approval and selection. I will say nothing except this: the candidate that was best fit for the position was not accepted by him. His candidate of choice was hired and selected against the recommendation of the department. I never understood Centrevia's infatuation

with Randall. For a while, I thought the organization was just going crazy
and then I realized that the system was such that connections and acceptance were more powerful than morals in the corporate world. Randall
and those like him soared.

I tried to understand and yet I saw hourly people let go because they
had an indiscretion such as flirting, DWI or a temper flare up. Others were
dismissed because of poor decisions and flirting with the wrong person. Yet
executives did this on a daily basis in their visible and leadership positions.
I began to face the fact that the masses are used by the system until the
system has no more need for their services. There was no protection for
them, but these executives were safe under the wings of the system. People
like Randall, who turned on the people that made them and mentored
them, will someday find out that they too were whored; they just got done
in the penthouse instead of in the low budget hotel.

Chapter 7

As a Public Interactions and Communications professional, the level of exposure to the company is vastly different than the line management view. I was quickly blown away at what I was seeing and I felt as though I had landed in the pit of hell again. For someone like me, who is the crusader for fair and equitable treatment, I was now in the nerve center of disarray. Public Relations under Centrevia was under the same corporate reporting structure as the Employee Relations System. With this pairing came exposure to the policies, guidelines and employee systems of the company. I had been through some difficult times through the years with this organization, but now I saw more of the deep wound that fed the surface sores. What I thought I would be a part of was the foundation and framework of the company, the brand and the employee life cycle.

Becoming one of the policy makers was a natural next step for me. I had built departments and managed employees, but now I would be in the company of those who administrate programs. It was to be a great season, like the dawning of spring. There were no birds singing or blooming fields of poppies. I landed in thorns.

After meeting the staff and getting settled, it became obvious to me that there was strife amongst the group. An unhealthy competition and unspoken guidelines ruled. It was not that people were not friendly; they were just compartmentalized and I did not find a united department. My belief had always been that attitude reflects the leadership and leadership affords positive behavior. The senior executives in Relational Functions included vice presidents and deputy officers of Public Relations and Employee Relations. I considered my executive, Steve Benjamin, to be light-hearted and approachable. What I did not know was that he was under the gun due to the overpowering C-suite executives who were circling him. I could not figure out if they liked him or not. They seemed to be accepting of him but not confident in him. His down line was involved with him but not particularly trusting of him. There were exceptions, including one who would take a bullet for him.

I began the new position with dreams in spite of the concerns. I had been doing double duty to assist Environmental Effects through its transition, so I was a little frazzled. I knew for sure that I had been whored now; there was no doubt. I now had access to the systems and I could see the history reports for executives from a variety of sites. I would have rather stayed ignorant. Even at the director level, my peers whom I had worked beside and often times advised were years ahead of me in salary. There in black and white was a sixty thousand dollar difference between my salary and most of my peers'. Not a ten, twenty or even thirty thousand difference, but *sixty thousand dollars?* In fact, I was the lowest paid at my level in the company. Now full circle, I could see where Centrevia derailed me over the years. I was exposed to one contradiction after the other and the darts and wounds I had experienced in the past years were gaping, open sores now. I wondered how many of my colleagues had put in the hours I had or developed as many people. How many had saved the company the money I had?

Exposure to the department also showed me that the company underwrote items for executives and their families. I have since learned this was common practice in the upper levels of the corporate structure. Anything could be justified under miscellaneous expenses, if you were in the right seat. Everything was apparently acceptable, from the internships that were designer-made for selected students while other deserving students were ignored, to special programs for spouses and dependents. Centrevia executives would even identify those individuals that were considered to be talented and afford them additional bonuses and merit raises, and I really hated that. I saw the raises of 10 and 20 percent given to some and 1 percent to others when the objectives were, in most cases, totally subjective. That meant the people working day and night to build, maintain and improve processes were not given the same considerations. The company supposedly wanted people with the best pedigree; you know, those from Ivy League universities. News flash: if this was really the case, it is interesting that a successful graduate of one of those Ivy League universities would find herself dismissed in a few months. Ironically, many of the executives of Centrevia had no degrees, while others certainly did not have "Ivy League Credentials."

The duties under my direction included several key areas. Over and over I submitted proposals for additional staff. Each time the requests were denied. I was asked to build a Public Interactions machine, but was given no staffing or support. In spite of that, I did build the program. I took the position to make a difference and to master yet another area of the company. My plan was now mastering the Public Interactions and Communications arena, which would build a profile that would enable me to move further up the executive track to build for my retirement. It was not the most important part of my life, but this would help my family and there were perks to the higher executive life. I had openly given my best to the company and I needed to recover financially from the years of expenses resulting from recent issues.

I was not naïve. I knew that like most corporate executives today, Centrevia senior and C-Suite executives received the big perks. There were luxury fleet cars, gas cards wherein all maintenance was taken care of; bonus levels were 30 to 50 percent of their salaries; and they were paid for considerable time off. Contrast this to the people at the lower end receiving 3 to 5 percent no matter how well the company performed. Just imagine not paying for a car or the insurance, gas, etc. on top of earning $250,000 as a minimum, with the sky being the limit at the high end, plus a bonus of 50 percent each year with guarantees in place that you could not be paid less than that. I remembered the people like the factory floor workers who made less than one-eighth of that salary and supported families every day. I had wiped the tears when they could not meet their bills and yet the company refused to institute a program to allow a one-time emergency grant of $500 to any employee who had been at the company for at least three years, or to allow a discount on food for those at the lower end. I wanted to tell the president and Congress that Intron, AIG or the automotive industries are not alone in killing the American dream. It is also companies like Centrevia, who pimp their employees and berate people by telling them that most of them deserved nothing for raises and bonuses. Constantly, the executives communicated that we are only after talent, and the steady, consistent workers who performed daily were not it. It was like a spouse telling their mate that although they are expected to perform in every way, the neighbor's spouse is far superior. We were told so many times to recruit talented people, only those fitting the company pedigree of the day.

We found, on countless occasions, an excellent candidate with experience and education that was perfect for a position, yet he or she was dismissed from consideration. It became routine for excellent candidates to be turned down once the details of the candidate became evident. Some applications were trashed right out of the blocks. The organization wanted a certain look and feel. Other candidates were turned away after being brought in for interview due to the physical characteristics of the individual. This became so alarming to me that I requested that we give an in-service to the department to remind everyone of the dangers of discrimination in any form. I continued to draw attention to the wrongs and my influence and performance were beginning to be challenged. I confided in my friends and family that I was under a lot of pressure and that no matter what I asked for, I got nothing in staff to help me with this crusade. In reality, as a good "system whore," I should have kept my mouth shut and stayed in the position. I tried but I just could not do that. I'm sorry; I'm a bad whore.

I was told a few weeks later that the department executive was getting pressure and was afraid that I was not the person for the position, unless I could prove him wrong by making some changes. This was so interesting because concerns were not cited until I began to expose issues. I was told that the programs that I instituted were not sound and despite the fact that they received excellent comments from the students, executives, other employees, as well as external representatives, the organization was not happy with me in the position. I was confused, since I had just received accolades from the president and executive staff regarding the excellent programs that I defined and implemented. Compounded was the fact that they continued to deny my request for staffing assistance. The message back to me again: "Bad whore, Anora, close mouth, empty your mind and assume the position." The answer to my immediate staffing situation was to get a trainee or intern. No staffing would be approved.

The following week I was scheduled for a meeting in Steve Benjamin's office to discuss progress on some key programs. I knew all along that this was not exactly going to be above board—just a hunch. As the meeting began, Steve began by telling me that the pressure he was under was tremendous. I, in turn, asked him who the pressure was coming from. I found him to be especially aloof that day. He went on to say that when he hired me as Director of Public Interactions, he had expectations that he now felt I could not meet, but he thought I was a wonderful person. I countered with the fact that after countless requests for the staff that was needed and after submitting five specific proposals, he had given me nothing. I was conducting all tasks myself. How strategic can a person be when all of this is on one set of shoulders? Yet I got it done.

With that he told me that he had decided to hire a new Director of Public Interactions. I countered that I did not realize we were looking for one, especially since I was in that position. He went on to say he had found a wonderful person that he just knew I was going to love. When people say that it usually means that there is something you have in common with the candidate. I found that people ususally say that when the candidate is ethnic or a woman. I knew it was not a woman, so he must not be white. And so he was. It appears that all this time, without the slightest hint to me, my executive and the executive team had been determined to replace me. And the replacement happened to be a younger man. Then he very quickly said that "we have a brand new role for you. We want you to take the lead in Institutional Relations and build this program and the others you were working on specifically. We know that this was just too much for one person."

Okay, now I was a little ticked off. So all along I had been asking for staffing because it was too much, and his answer to my proposals for staffing was to demote me and get in someone over me, and I get to keep my duties with a very public raping of title? All that time he told me there was no headcount; he could find the headcount to bring in this person and he could not give me the staff initially promised? Calmly, I asked, "And what is my title level, since this person will be my boss?"

"Well now," he said, "you will get to keep your level." This caused great concern for me, because I know the business and organizational structure, but more importantly I know the hand of Centrevia. He took great time to reassure me that my position was safe. This meant that as a director, I would report to another director. In corporate America this is know as a demotion. In life it would be called "suckered."

What Steve Benjamin did was further help me to see that there was no one I could trust at Centrevia, and now I had a new boss and another layer between me and my executive line. Orlando Moreno was his name and to hear Steve talk, he found him to be wonderful. In my mind I was wondering why I should care. I asked him this: "What makes you think that I am going to love someone who I already know, by pattern of the organization, is younger than I am and makes much more money?"

Then he said, "Anora, he's also a minority hire. He is part black and part Latino/Hispanic."

I informed him that every ethnic person does not take a definite liking to every other ethnic person or to everyone who has ethnic heritage. If that was true, then every white person would just love and want to be around everyone who had Caucasian heritage. I think not. We are as different as you are and we have preferences too. Minorities, races and ethnicity may involve common characteristics, and yes, there should be pride for people with common heritage, but we are not linked by some divine law to be each other's biggest fan. Frankly, the greatest bond I find in people is those that share my belief in Jesus Christ. So many times he had said that color does not matter. Then why continue to hold it as a banner? It works both ways. He was trying to smooth over an underhanded deed by using the reverse color card. "Look he's a lot like you . . . he's part black—now doesn't that hurt a little less?" If I had done it, you would say I was using the race card. It is a lie that people do not see color when they look at other people, unless you are physically colorblind. What should be the truth, however, is that you embrace the differences and realize that all are accepted. This was not the issue here. He was hired, I was demoted and both of us were minorities so "you do not lose in the end. Your statistics are a wash." The fact is, it did not matter to me in that moment.

With the announcement of a new Director of Public Interactions coming, I was baffled as to what exactly Orlando was going to do that I could not do. Why was Steve determined to bring him in and toss me aside? I was not born yesterday and I knew that there was always a real story behind the movements in the corporate world. Word was out and people were treating me as though I had been stricken with a disease. There were silent pats on the back to say "I am so sorry." My colleagues would say, "Well look at it this way. He can take the heat and you will just have an easier existence. You get to keep your money that's all that matters." No. There's more that matters.

It took a long time for Steve to announce Orlando's coming to the organization. I, on the other hand, was going about my day-to-day activities; what else could I do? All the executives knew that I had ultimately been demoted and replaced and none seemed to care that the move was a professional insult. I think my biggest disappointment was when I approached the CEO. He asked me if I was all right with the changes. Note to self: a corporate pimp cares not that you are being abused and screwed, even though he has the power to stop the rape. Hearing him ask me how I felt about it was like asking me if it hurt when I had a mastectomy. To be demoted and treated in this manner was an insult, a slap in the face that hit in the same spot. This same man celebrated the programs and accolades I had brought to the company with a celebration dinner four months ago. He then went on to talk about how Steve thought so highly of this new person and he had full confidence that he would radically improve the area, and that I, on the other hand, would be able to concentrate on what I love best. How would he know what I love best? What he meant was "Be quiet, Anora, and take what we give you. Close your mouth and assume the position. Do what you are told." I wanted to leave Centrevia; I should have.

Weeks had passed and the day had now come to meet Orlando. I reasoned to myself that this man was not guilty; he had no way of knowing that he was coming into this mess. I was sure that the picture painted for him was different and more than likely he did not know of my time with the organization. When we met, I knew that he was not aware of the Centrevia reality, but then I was not necessarily the one who should tell him. He was a corporate PR guy, but as we talked, he really was a nice guy.

In all actuality, Orlando and I got along fine, but again that was my nature and seemingly his. I did everything and I showed him the ropes. I gave him all the knowledge I could about the company and processes because I know how this place works. No disrespect to him, but in truth to the organization, the old whores teach the younger whores and in time selected by the system, the old whores are thrown away. I had not figured the timing out but I knew that. We continued to work and I realized that Orlando had something I did not have that would make his programs successful. He had me to assist him. He had the staff I had asked for. Ironically, I sent him the proposals I had previously submitted for staffing and just as I thought, the proposal was blessed as brilliant and he was given more headcount.

Going forward I documented everything about the company: unjustified decisions, behind-the-scenes sexual affairs, harassment, everything. A disturbing pattern within the department was gaining even more momentum with the total disregard for several members of the staff.

In October of that year, Steve Benjamin resigned his executive position. He left fairly unannounced and speculation was that he was asked to leave, but of course he was compensated well. In a few weeks, the announcement was made that a new senior executive of Relational Function was hired. Stan Powers was now in the seat and as was usual, when the power shifted, the jockeying for favoritism began and it became evident that he had already been informed on how to proceed. Stan was in place for three weeks when he announced reorganization of the department. He took into his confidence a member of the staff who was working diligently to get into Stan's inner circle.

The next few weeks were filled with behind-the-scenes meetings in and out of the executives' offices. It was also evident that several other members of the staff knew something and began to play this really strange cat and mouse game. I knew there would be a change in my status because I became even further shunned by anyone in the organization with power or influence. This was very Centrevia-like, to allow such a conflict of interest where peers to the people being let go knew the particulars before the victims. Things were starting to leak out and another employee took me into confidence that I was mentioned as one of the people under consideration to be let go. When? A few days later, I found myself in an elevator, on my way to the CEO's office.

When the elevator closed, I was surprised by my feelings and I just stood there looking at the buttons. If I pressed the button, my twenty-year career with Centrevia would end. But still, if I pressed nothing, someone else would eventually summon the elevator and press a button for his destination, and my twenty-year career would still end. Ten women from the department were being let go. We had families, homes, children, and many obligations. None of us were slackers. Over and over, we were told that this was not personal. Tell that to those depending on us. We would become displaced people who find their paychecks and benefits gone. There was a strategy behind the reorganization and anyone could see it. Some who remained were new to the company. They were young and inexperienced. Others were better aligned to those in the decision-making positions. But remember: "whore" today, gone tomorrow. Releasing all of us under the false justification that our positions were eliminated? People were hired in all these positions. One was the twenty-three-year-old son of a senior executive's best golfing buddy and vacation friend. Another was a young woman hired into a support position who became friendly with several key executives. There were many stories. I was concerned most for those whose emotions were difficult to contain after finding out the news. I became the voice of calm. How? I don't know. Actually, I take that back; I do know. It was only through the loving hand of a merciful God.

There on that day, I had no choice, no voice and soon no job. To add insult to the situation, Orlando told me that instead of having my last day as scheduled, our new VP insisted that I leave early. I was given fifteen minutes to leave my office and finalize my twenty years of service to Centrevia. I knew my time was ending, but in my mind I was prepared to leave with my dignity intact. I had planned to say goodbyes and get closure by seeing the people. I simply loved them. So with Orlando nearby, I felt like a criminal, and the clock was ticking . I found the strength to compose an exit email. I sent it to all in the mailing system but I meant it only for some. This was no longer my company. I no longer existed here. There was no more Anora Bradley in the eyes of the corporation.

> From: BRADLEYAnora [mailto:Anora.Bradley@Centrevia.com]
> Subject: Farewell and I wish you well
> Dear Centrevia Colleagues,
> It is with deep gratitude that I send you this message and I hope that you know what my time working with you has meant. You are like family to me, as we have worked, laughed, and cried together. Your professionalism and dedication will forever be engraved in my heart.
> Many of you have shared my life and prayed with me through the tough times. I thank you for that, and you know that my heart is true and my loyalty to you will always be there. Even in this time of change, I have great peace in knowing that all is well.
> I wish you much success and leave here knowing that we accomplished great things of which I had a part. I now join the legacy of dedicated, talented professionals who have moved on and, in turn, devoted themselves to our collective success.
> To those of you who wish to contact me, my personal e-mail address is attached. Know that I am proud to have been your colleague, your manager, director, mentor and friend. There is much greatness to come. . . .
> With deep admiration,
> Anora N. Bradley

So I asked to be alone for a few moments and I prepared to leave. I prayed for the people at Centrevia and I asked God to protect them; well, most of them. If I could turn the hands of time back I would have done things so differently. I would have qualified my career without the invest-ment of my full self. One of the first lessons I tell young people is to set their work pace according to the price they are willing to pay, and never lose any aspect of yourself in the day-to-day work life. The vortex will suck you dry if you allow the suckers to attach to you. What that does not mean is to waste today. It simply means that if you go through today without awareness of your investment, you have overspent and will in some way, someday overdraft your reserve, whether it is energy, creativity or health. There are times in life when you must accelerate and get it done quickly. Just be sure that what you are racing to does not devour you. Corporate America has its way of morphing itself and emitting the sweet smell of what we are conditioned to think of as success. It is caustic.

Chapter 8

My exit meeting was one of the most demeaning events of my life and I sat across from a stone-faced colleague carrying on the mission he was assigned. Charles Willis had become an appendage of the machine. He had accepted whatever the assignment was in exchange for knowing that he would keep his job. This is happening in many companies, the breeding ground of the "save yourself, get all you can" mentality, and many have perfected the art. Most people need to work and many are forced to be prostitutes of the system in one way or another. When the pimp says turn your trick, you turn it. Charles was the choice whore of the day, but he was not the only one.

Centrevia did not care about the fact that I was a significant contributor of income for my family, nor that my husband and I were only a few years beyond our life-threatening illnesses and multiple surgeries. Insurance for us due to preexisting conditions—without the benefit of an employer's plan—was a huge financial challenge and no guarantee under most subscribers. Why would these executives take a moment to think about the fact that their role in this situation afforded me an exit that was fitting to a criminal and not a twenty-year veteran of the industry? The tone in my exit interview was degrading and insulting, a fine ending to my career.

What we, as people, are experiencing in the workplace are not layoffs and anyone castrated from his or her career knows this. A layoff, by definition of the word, means that you lay something down or use motion to displace it. What is happening in the corporate world today is forced prostitution followed by career castration. It is truly the nonconsensual removal of employees from the workplace by whatever means are necessary in order to increase the bottom line. We have seen it over and over again in the past few years and unfortunately it continues. The few taps on the bottom given to corporations have not deterred it. Instead, it simply taught the C-suite pimps how to camouflage their actions. Some say that the economy is picking up and we simply must wait it out. Wait out what? In these new employment sagas, after the company ends employment, the new situation is that if you get severance, the time period is but a fraction of what it used to be and benefits are, in many cases, not included. When you have medical issues and are responsible for the insurance for your family, you have now lost more than some people can bear. Your income is gone and your medical care, including any transition and ongoing care, is now eliminated.

The frustration here is that many of my colleagues and I were let go not because of performance, insubordination, inappropriate behavior or anything related. We were "let go" because the company decided to release us. All of us were intelligent and in many cases we were the company's front-line voice or experience through the darkest and toughest days. The reward for our work, our effort and our sacrifice was abandonment. This is the new creed of the corporate world. It is neither about the employee nor the contributions they have made. Instead, it is about the ability of the C-suite executives to roll the dice and completely redirect people's lives.

In this generation of self-help books and talk shows, I'm sure there is a twelve-step recovery program for prostitutes who are pimped by the predators of the streets, some mantra based on the Serenity Prayer, or another inspirational prose. But where is the recovery program for educated professionals victimized by the seductive, corporate-choreographed movements endearingly known as the path to success? We, the masses, are pimped by the business suit, the blackberry and the boardroom. We are the successful professionals proven to get the job done, all the while surrendering to corporate America just as a prostitute to the pimp. So many of us were bound by society's expectations and our unrealistic dreams of professional and personal success.

I struggled for years to identify what I was seeing happen to employees in the company. For years, we thought that the paychecks we were earning were the result of a company paying us for the work we provided. In all reality we came to the final realization that we were pimped by the system that controlled our success. People in the midst of adversity do not become fully aware of what has transpired until they begin to recover. In the aftermath of crisis, one does not realize the magnitude of the trauma. I did not know the price I paid while working those long hours and sacrificing my health and so much of my life. Clearly, I did not let my family long for anything and I took care of everything and everyone—except myself. When you are driving down the road and suddenly the unexpected happens, you find out who and what you really are. So many things go through your mind when the company you trusted tells you that you are no longer needed. To them, you are simply a number; do not fool yourself. The pyramid of many companies in corporate America is only concerned with feeding the top and unfortunately the food on which they dine is made up of the people down below. It hurt but I had to face that truth.

All those years I was simply spent, used, and "pimped." I stand admitting that I was prostituted. Who knew that I would someday be what I feared most? That I would look around one day and find that I was unemployed and looking for a position at fifty-three years old? It had been over twenty years since I had to look for employment. If not for my belief in God, I would have succumbed to the depression that has overtaken so many. I even went through a period where I tried to rationalize that some of the executives in the company cared about me and that they tried to fight for me. They stood valiantly and defended the fact that Anora Bradley must stay! They rallied to show the departments that were built, and the tens of millions of dollars of optimizations, improvements and solutions that resulted! They stood united to say that the doors of Centrevia welcomed this champion for the employees, and her leadership and mentoring developed empowerment and effective employees for many years! They did this for me . . . didn't they? Surely they did, considering that I helped each of them at work and even in personal situations. I nursed one of the executives, who was here without a family, through the flu, including cleaning up after him and bringing food to his bedside. Anora Bradley toured children, wives, parents and friends around town when there were crises in executives' lives. I was there for everything, their celebrations and their tragedies. The pearls of my wisdom and the songs of my laughter adorned and embraced them. Like a virtuous woman routed in loyalty and love, I stood by them. Yet today, I know that none spoke on my behalf. None gave account of the woman I am. No words of support were whispered.

I always knew that it could happen and I saw it happen. I knew where the bodies were buried. I knew all the secrets of the company, yet I never thought they would risk all that I knew. Now, I am not one to hold that over their heads, but really? Letting me go after all that I had done and all those years was a tragedy. I am not saying that I was some kind of hero, but I was the people's champion. And then I took a really good look around and I noticed that the only people saddened by my dismissal were those not in high managerial or executive capacity. In fact, for the last few weeks, executives had been avoiding me like the plague. When they needed something from me, they would send their requests through others. I knew something was up but I really thought they would offer me a position in another capacity. I knew that my age was against me as I had heard the conversation and been tipped off. I just thought that it would still be okay.

I was reminded of a scene from an old movie. The woman that raised the slave owner's children had resolved herself to the fact that her deeds would afford her the certainty that the master would not sell her own children, because she was treated like family. She fed and nurtured the master's children and she was his bed partner for years in her capacity as a possession. But then one day, out of nowhere, her child was sold. She begged and pleaded and appealed to the master, reminding him of all those years when her body was his pleasure. She listed all the things she had done and the love she had shown his children and even his wife. But then, in that moment, she realized that she was, in fact, just property to him. Painfully she discovered that the children, her womb, her body and her time were all taken at will, just like the work of our hands, our creativity, our talents and our devotion to the company were pimped by the company. When this is truly realized, there is a pain that radiates to our inner self. The violation that you know is that your value was only to promote the cause for a season. Even deeper is the real pain, that we allowed this to happen. I relaxed my boundaries and before I knew it, I thought I was in a family. I lost consciousness of the fact that the company is not a person; instead, it is an institution run by a few people at the top. Hear me that this is not every company, but those not fitting the equation are few.

Since leaving Centrevia, I started a network marketing business, among other things, and I find it striking that people often ask why I'm involved in a pyramid scheme. How amusing that these are the same people that work in these companies. A pyramid, by definition, is a shape that affords a large bottom and becomes increasingly narrow at the top. That is, in fact, corporate structure. The masses at the bottom are the workers, employees that by the sweat of the brow, works of the hand, and immersion of the mind, work for wage and salary set by strict guidelines enforced by those at the top. The top levels of the company are only a few people with all power and decision-making responsibilities. In the corporate world, those at the bottom of the structure will never ascend to the coveted top of the structure and will never enjoy the benefits, perks or salary of those at the top. That is the true pyramid of the corporate world.

And so I am learning to find my worth again, but I wonder if the executives at Centrevia know the pain they have caused in my life and the lives of others discarded by their machine. Do they ever think about the insurance that is beyond an affordable price, or the fact that at fifty-three the job market does not welcome you? I passed by one of the executives the other day in his corporate car and I remembered the projects and meetings we worked on, the bonuses and perks he was getting and the many special requests I assisted him with. He was always a nice person in my presence, but he was also the person that signed to approve my dismissal. Many times I thought about all the things I knew, the things that haunted me about Centrevia. I have no regrets for bringing the company's attention to issues. I lived by a code and I do not regret that. What I regret is not leaving when the first red flags waved. So many betrayals . . .

In a perfect world, there would be reward for anyone able to work hard and remain honest. There would be no desire to prosper at anyone's expense. This world is not perfect. Our expectation was to go to school and get a good job with a company so that our families could live comfortably. In the process of achieving this, the rules shifted. Our society required more and more of us to maintain a life and afford a family, and we became enslaved to the companies that afforded us the paycheck. When some companies realized that there was no consequence, they openly become the Corporate Pimp. The blame is not all on them. We must take ownership of the fact that we allowed ourselves to be pimped. When the pimp reigns, the whore must maintain the work that feeds them both until freed either by choice, chance, or sheer will. Either way, a new life can emerge if desire is strong enough.

Chapter 9

On my last day at Centrevia, Orlando walked me to my car. I was emotionally bruised but I fought my heart and demanded that my body make no tears, none. There would be no lasting, tearful exit story to tell. I had watched and heard too many emotional stories of employees breaking down and even begging to stay. I needed no escort from the building and I wanted the chance to turn this intended walk of shame into a trot of freedom. As Orlando walked beside me, I stopped midway to my car and looked at him long and hard. I looked at the campus around me and drank in the beauty of a wonderful May afternoon in Virginia. Even after the events of the day, God allowed me to see the beauty and the fact that no man or manmade institution could take any of it away.

I turned to Orlando and let him know that I was going to be just fine, and perhaps even better than ever, so there was absolutely nothing for him to be concerned about. On the other hand, I knew that it would take a power greater than me to mend the damage inside me. Stan emerged from the main entrance and told me that he wanted to catch me before leaving. He gave me the "On behalf of Centrevia, thank you for your service" bit. I listened to his final speech about what I had done and the mark I made on the company. It actually sounded like he was eulogizing my career. There is a parallel there, because a part of my life died on that day. I would never again trust my career and so much of myself to the hands of anyone. I had learned what my position, salary and benefits had really cost me, and the price was too high.

I was not saying that I would never work for a company again, because I need to bring money into my household. What I was admitting is that God would gather the pieces that were left to remake me. I never doubted God — I had come through family loss, illness and many challenges — but I underestimated the pain and shame associated with losing a long-term job and my career. I had let myself become much too vulnerable. You do become hypnotized, and as a result, you have a distorted view of what and who the company is to you. I had to educate myself to understand that I am not what I do, I am who I am, and that applies to all aspects of my life. When, by force or persuasion, you become what you do, your power is severely limited. I heard someone once say that you must separate your who from your do. In order to begin recovery, I needed to give birth to new dreams and put my twenty-year career in its place. I could never return to Centrevia, and the many relationships that I had built had to be reevaluated to determine their worth outside the company. The painful reality was that the reputation I thought I had was no longer intact. The company damaged my professional credibility. I was told that because I was well-loved by those who had worked for me and with me over the years, my departure caused an uprising of emotion. Thus, the executives and CEO requested that I be asked to leave prior to my dismissal date. I had no time to say the goodbyes that I needed for closure and the unscheduled exit left some thinking that I did something wrong. I did do something wrong; I left myself on the vine too long and almost allowed my dreams to rot. Just in time, I was ejected from the vine by the merciful hand of a loving God. What was meant for my harm was turned into my good.

Recovery would not come easy for me because I associated my dismissal from the company with betrayal, almost as if a spouse cheated. I had to search myself to realize that this was not the case. There was no unconditional love from the company for me. I had a purpose and once that was served, I was expendable. It was business at Centrevia and it not only applied to me but other respected colleagues. I had to face the workplace reality that pimps do not love their whores. Rather, they love what their whores can do for them. The most difficult time was ahead in that my confidence was rocked.

When I ran into people from Centrevia just after my dismissal, I made sure that they saw the brave face and confident person that I pretended to be. I hid the tears and rejection that Ben, Daniel and Tia saw. The stress of being laid off began to take its toll on my relationships in strange ways. My faith was not shaken, but my immediate reactions to life were skewed due to my depth of rejection. I talked to many people that were laid off and the range of emotions was as wide as the sky. On any given day my emotions ran the full span of anger, bewilderment, and pure and simple abandonment. I watched the news one night and found that I was no longer wondering why some people do things like return to the workplace and commit acts that are shocking to many. I thank God that I am centered in faith and that I can control the urge to seek my own vengeance. I have no need for that, nor should anyone. Losing it that way solves nothing. We were a threat to our pimps and that is not tolerated on the streets or the boardroom. We were forthright. The list was long and the company was willing to dismiss years of experience, which will ultimately come back to haunt them as the days issues return. I have no malice; I release them to a higher power. Control is the currency of exchange in the hands of the Corporate Pimp. I made my last deposit.

I have searched myself and I know now that there are choices even when there appears there are none. It is a fact that no matter what the circumstances, no one and no entity can take the right we have to remain true to ourselves. I never thought that I would understand the hopelessness that people contemplating suicide feel, or the rage that people who take vengeance feel. I just never really thought about it. Ironically, it took not an act of violence, illness, or even a broken heart to show me that I could come close to a feeling of helpless rejection. Strangely, it took the abandonment of my income potential to do that. It took a while, but I finally realized why. Love of family and God were always in place for me and I gave my unconditional love to those relationships. God and family are my core and I thank God this is what sustained me. We all need an income to live and as long as there is the need for money on this earth, even the good, the committed and the sound of mind and character can become pimped. I have learned that I have no choices in my yesterday, but I have every choice in my present and my future. I am not for sale, lease or rent ever again, consciously or unconsciously. I am creative, loving and intelligent with a bounty of gifts from God. I know that my worth is not in my doing; it is in my being, and my being belongs to no man.

Chapter 10

In the midst of adversity we do not become fully aware of what has transpired until we begin to recover. In the direct aftermath of a crisis, one does not realize the magnitude of the trauma. Here I am, Anora Bradley, kneeling at the altar of no more corporate job, no more formal paycheck and a nonexistent professional identity; I was brought to the mirror to see myself. When you are driving down the road and suddenly the unexpected happens, you cannot always predict your response. That is why it is so vital that you identify your vulnerable areas, prepare for those things that you can control, and release the ultimate "all" to God.

I faced myself in a way I had never dreamt of at this point in life. Who knew I would someday be the very person I devoted my life to protecting? I became one of the violated, the purposely seduced, and I allowed it to happen. I stayed too long like fruit on the tree. You know—like that beautiful apple as it ripens from bitter green to a red, delicious, juicy delight that must be picked at just the right time. If left on the tree, that lovely treat softens and drops to the ground, bruised and rotting. Slowly, it becomes nothing. There are lessons to learn.

All of a sudden I looked at myself and began a conversation like none other I had ever had. It was as though I was talking to another person. "Hello Anora. I find you looking at me often and I know that when our eyes meet, there is a kindness and understanding. Why are you avoiding me? If you take a moment you will see strength meet vulnerability, so stop running from what you really feel. On any given day there are moments when I want to tell you some things, but I can't. There is so much inside me right now that I sometimes feel as if I can no longer contain this from the world. Funny, huh? God already knows. If only there was a way to release some of the absolute truth inside me. I can't because I don't think the world could handle it nor would I want my family to have to come to grips with all the feelings I have. No, it's just easier to live with it and continue limiting myself." And then I stopped to breathe.

My conversation went on and I told myself that I know that someday, there would be a day for dreams and realizing that my career success was never dependent on the corporate world. I was always meant to exist outside of the cage. All of a sudden I simply and drastically began to laugh out loud to see a woman in the mirror instead of an unrecognizable being. So let's take a re-do on this. "Remember what Mama Hattie told you? What you wake up wanting to do and what you would do absolutely free—those are your passions. You separated your career life from the things that gave you passion in your spiritual life. That was a mistake. Take the same direction with both; God has been telling you that all along—you were never created to be a prostitute to any system." I gave everything in me to this effort. My energy, brain power, resolve, my intellect and so much more: pimped. Working at Centrevia occupied too much of my existence. So I stopped trying and left that life behind. I began to search for the passions I buried.

A few months later, on a warm summer evening with smells of cumin and lavender on the restaurant patio I stood. I could hear the faint sounds of those people in the main dining area as dinner reservations were beginning. I just stopped for a moment to feel the evening breeze and I loved the vines that grew on the patio lattice. The candles were all lit and I felt so inspired standing in this very spot. I brought my family here a few months ago. I loved it. I just did. The combination of food, people, nature, the wines of life all here for the taking . . . it was like one of my sweet spots. My son Daniel called those areas on the basketball court where his special shots sank through the net his sweet spots. This place was one of mine. I had others, but this was one.

I returned to the kitchen to prepare for a large party that would arrive within the hour. It was another business dinner that, at our place, would turn into a magically relaxing experience of tastes, smells, and family. Here, everyone felt like a family. After all, the table is the altar of the home. We had many tables and all who broke bread here were nurtured and enjoyed. We started the sauces and organized for the evening party. As the orders came in, I was almost intoxicated by the smells of each dish. A few months can make a big difference in a person's life. Today, surrounded by one of my true loves, I was thankful.

As the evening progressed, the waiter asked that the chefs come out to greet a party of executives. The appetizers and main course had been served. It was an experience in dining that they had not experienced before. What was it about this place? So we went to meet the party after preparing a masterpiece of dessert and coffee. Cora the Head Chef, as is customary, went first and I followed. Winding out to the private patio, my steps slowed when I saw the familiar faces ahead. I stood to the rear and listened to Cora interact with the executives of Centrevia. "Thank you" and "Please enjoy," she told them. There, in that moment, enjoying the excellent work of our hands, were the satisfied customers of my talents. My culinary art was just one of my self-nourishing ventures. By this point, I also had a thriving network marketing business and my work with the church, community, and children. I am a rich and blessed woman. My name is Anora, and a short time ago I lived a life chained to a system, where I did not belong. I am blessed.